Praise for

An Empty Room

"A confident and piquant first novel about first loves."
—*The Herald* (United Kingdom)

"A beautifully written debut." —*Heat* (United Kingdom)

"An authentic evocation of a young woman on the cusp of self-discovery." —*The Big Issue* (United Kingdom)

"*An Empty Room* echoes with the dreamy unreality of a hot summer night." —*The Observer* (United Kingdom)

"A stunning debut . . . An exquisite, stylishly written novel."
—*Irish Examiner*

"A taut, immensely engaging novel from the outset. Pure, but certainly not simplistic, it draws the reader into a claustrophobic world of first love angst and delivers a satisfying and mature ending. A compelling, brilliant debut, written without a wasted word, it tackles well-trodden territory in an original and poignant way."
—Whitbread First Novel Award Judges Panel

"Stevenson writes with grace and precision. *An Empty Room* is a lovely book, an absolutely clear and pitiless study of the human heart and its capacities for love, betrayal, and finally, forgiveness."

—Nicole Stansbury, author of *Places to Look for a Mother*

"*An Empty Room* is about the obsession and languor of the almost adult, and is written with honesty and an element of wistfulness which combine in a voice that is clear and true."

—Raffaella Barker, author of *Summertime*

An Empty Room

Also by Talitha Stevenson

Exposure

TALITHA STEVENSON

An Empty Room

A HARVEST BOOK
HARCOURT, INC.
Orlando Austin New York
San Diego Toronto London

www.HarcourtBooks.com

First U.S. edition published by Carroll & Graf, 2004

Library of Congress Cataloging-in-Publication Data
Stevenson, Talitha.
An empty room/Talitha Stevenson.
p. cm.
"A Harvest Book."
1. Young women—Fiction. 2. Single women—Fiction.
3. Parent and adult child—Fiction. 4. Adultery—Fiction.
5. England—Fiction. I. Title.
PR6119.T48E47 2005
823′.92—dc22 2005046397
ISBN-13: 978-0156-03281-0 ISBN-10: 0-15-603281-3

Text set in Aldus

Printed in the United States of America

First Harvest edition 2005
K J I H G F E D C B A

For my amazing mother,
Nicola Stevenson

An Empty Room

Chapter one

Tom's hands were never still. There is a whole film reel of them in my mind. They picked his initials into wooden tables, they made wine glasses sing, struck matches one after the other, tore up beer mats, drummed on coffee tables, they even turned on each other until the skin was picked sore around the nails. At first I sympathised with those hands, they implied imagination, they were like me: full of love, disappointment, mania. But they wouldn't let anything alone. Nothing was sacred in the end, except the hands themselves. If I move my tongue to the right of my mouth I can feel they have smashed out one of my teeth.

I was once told by the family counsellor, a woman called Julia with red hair and a large mole on her right eyelid, that I have a problem engaging with a situation. Apparently, I have a tendency to 'intellectualise'.

'You hold yourself three feet above other people and you can't feel anything from up there – not pain or love either,' she said.

Well, I did feel love. I felt love which sent everyone else in the world home early and quietly switched out the lights. I felt love and now I've felt hate and violence. You could say I've been brought down to earth: you can't 'engage' more with a situation than being spread out on the floor, grit in your hair, splinters from the door frame under your fingernails and the taste of your own blood in your mouth. Slammed into the here and now, you'd have thought. I'd have thought . . . Funny though, how a smack in the face will get you thinking about destiny.

Pick a moment, any moment. Pretend each part contains the whole – because maybe it does. I could pick Tom's hands and the ice spinning in the glass, if I wanted to. I could tell Sarah was watching his hands too, because her parents were only away for the weekend and there was that pale carpet just underneath all that red drink. And Tom must have felt us watching him, but he was sure enough of his own stage presence to hold us for a while. After a bit, Sarah said:

'Tom? You haven't met Emily, have you?' and he looked up and smiled. It was a smile which only included me – a trick he later told me he had learnt from his father.

I was only going to stay for about an hour – I am a year older than Sarah and that evening I felt too grown-up for parties like that; the muted TV screen, the smoky mouths, the hot, transparent seduction by the empty bathroom.

'I'm a bit stressed about how many people there are,' Sarah said. 'There are people doing lines on the drawing-room mirror, for fuck's sake. I'm not going to say anything – I mean, you know me – but it's not like there isn't anything valuable in this house. That's the thing.'

She looked down and studied her fingers, her rings. You could see she was pleased: it was 4 a.m., everyone was drunk and happy and they were still using the ashtrays. Tom held up his hands the way thieves do:

'Hey, don't look at me.' Obviously people usually did. 'I don't know half these people, anyway.'

Sarah took a cigarette out of the packet in his shirt pocket and he looked up at me:

'Were you two at school together, then?'

'Emily was in the year above, Tom. She's my older, more glamorous friend. She's been off sending postcards from Italy and Spain, lucky thing, while I've been fucking up my exams.'

'Oh, you'll get straight As,' I said.

'Who knows? Anything could happen.'

'Not to you.'

'Great, I sound really interesting.' Sarah was never going to be happy.

'I just meant you plan things too well.'

'Do I?'

'Fancy planning things for me, Sarah?'

'Oh Tom, I couldn't possibly – your chaos is so *glamorous*.'

Glamorous was her favourite word. She was a jealous person who made very sure her compliments were cheap.

Right away I thought Tom was beautiful looking. He is someone women don't take their eyes off. He has sandy brown hair which gets in his eyes; he has a wide mouth and a long stretch – all loose belt and brown stomach – which is the golden prelude to any opinion he gives. I thought he looked spoilt the moment I saw him. He looked like he had a mother who was always telling him he was going to be famous.

After a while, the other people had gone and the door was closed – I can't really remember who closed it, maybe it was me. The music was echoing in from the other room and a thin tissue of smoke had gathered above the floor. Every now and then a shout of laughter would bloom through the wall or under the door and sometimes there was the faint sound of something breaking. Tom and I talked to each other for a while – about nothing, really: university, jobs, not really being able to picture it, and then he said something like:

'So, come here, then,' and kissed me – as if it was a conclusion to what we were saying. He kissed me very gently and when I looked back at him, at the fashionable clothes and the sharp, reckless posture, I thought it was not what I had expected.

Tom and I had been seeing each other for a few weeks when we realised our parents had known each other. Tom's father had finally left his mother just three months before, but when they had first got married, they lived in my parents' house. My parents were actually the same age as his – they had been at university together – but at twenty-five, when most young couples were still renting, Mum had inherited enough money to buy a house in Holland Park. Tom's parents had rented the big room in the basement, which was now a second sitting room.

'I can't believe you're still living there,' Tom said. 'The same walls for like twenty-three years. God, I never want to get like that.' He shivered and handed me a cigarette. Tom was stupid about a lot of things. He had been to six different schools and lived in three different countries before he was sixteen. He spoke three languages, but until he turned thirteen, he was not fluent in any one of them – even English. I could not imagine what that would be like. He still searched for the right word in one or the other of his languages, found it didn't translate. It made him seem lost – that and the slight, untraceable accent, the magazine unreality of his good looks.

His father had made a lot of money as a screenwriter and, following his dream of renovating a huge, noble old wreck, they had moved from beautiful place to beautiful place, each one falling short of the dream. Tom's childhood had been spent watching Romance tripped up and laughed at by Plumbing and Damp and Sewage. And he told the stories well – made his family sound like fanatics on the quest for the Holy Grail. He rolled his eyes and I wondered if there was something sophisticated about him – or if he had just picked it up from a film.

'You're not going to believe this,' he said, 'but my mum just bought the place opposite. We're neighbours.' He laughed, but I knew he wasn't joking. I suppose I didn't think Tom had much imagination, then. They were doing the place up, he told me, it would be ready in a few months.

We had been seeing each other nearly every day and he had started saying he loved me after we had sex (did I *realise* he had never said that before? Did I?) which always makes me feel lonely. I looked at him looking at me and wondered if I would ever feel like that about anyone. I thought we should probably see less of each other and I didn't feel sure I wanted him living over the road. I always pick watchers. Something in me attracts men you can picture back-lit and broad-shouldered in doorways, facing betrayal.

The house opposite ours had had a sign outside it for nearly a year and I noticed now it wasn't there. The people who lived there before, a Lebanese couple, had huge plans for it and had knocked walls through and gutted it. For a while there were always builders there working and the wife had put friendly 'sorry' notes through the letterbox about all the drilling. The husband used to sit on the doorstep with the builder talking over the plans which they weighed down on the ground in front of them with pieces of brick. Sometimes the wife would crouch behind and rest her arms on his shoulders. From my bedroom window, I thought it looked exciting to be married.

And then suddenly they left – no one knew why, but it must have been something terrible. I cried about all their plans. The house sat there naked and hungry looking, as if it had had a fantastic meal described to it, until Tom's mother came along and bought it. Perhaps she recognised the atmosphere there after giving up on so many places herself.

When I told my mother she looked really worried; her face folded up into its defining expression and she said '*An*drea and *To*ny?' to make absolutely sure. Then she said, 'Well, we'd better have them for dinner' – as if there was no choice. This is the way my mother approaches life. I said:

'They're not together any more, actually,' and she put down the tea towel and looked out of the window. After a while she said:

'Doesn't surprise me. He's an odd man.'

'Odd' in my mother's lexicon means anyone who doesn't

believe in God. She can handle different gods, but she can't understand no God – she doesn't know where to start with someone who lives only for the here and now. I watched her taking the things from the dishwasher and putting them into their places in the cupboard and I loved her and felt sorry for her.

My family is the kind that has books instead of tables, books instead of door-stops, books instead of footrests, drinks mats, intimacy. Instead of speaking to us, Dad quotes foreign literature. You know he's feeling potent if he's speaking in Italian poetry. None of us know the languages. It's comic, really – Dad sitting there at the table, eyes misted over, making big sounds which don't mean anything, while my sister and my mother and I wait to finish what's on our plates. My mother has never commented, and you'd have thought she just didn't notice, but a while ago, when some of her friends asked her to do an evening class with them, she said she just didn't think she was bright enough to learn French. Dad quoted something pertinent from Dante.

You only hear my younger sister's voice when she is on the telephone. Sometimes she says sad, little things to me, though. A while ago she said:

'Can we have a serious talk?' I said yes and we closed my door.

'I'm pretty sure I stink,' she said. Her toes were all bent back in the carpet.

'You don't.'

'It's a terrible smell,' she said. 'It's like when the rabbit died.' Ellie frightens herself – so I gave her my bottle of perfume. She smokes joints in her room and she's right not to worry, because my parents would never notice. Noticing is a complicated act, I have found out.

My parents don't notice anything. They never have. My mother didn't notice that my dad was having an affair. The woman was the wife of a Polish colleague of his from the university. Dad used to have me on Sunday mornings when Mum did Holy Communion classes. We always went to see Irena.

'I thought you might like to go and see Tomasz,' Dad used to say. He would be holding my coat, checking himself in the hall mirror. He would smell of sweet aftershave. I used to nod.

Tomasz was Irena's son. He was allergic to wheat and cheese and nuts. His eyes watered. We were the same age. We always had hot chocolate and every time she gave it to us, Irena would say: 'I'm a terrible mother – honestly, what this stuff does to your teeth, apart from anything else.' And Dad would tell her not to worry so much, that she was always worrying about everything. Tomasz and I would drink the hot chocolate quickly – sometimes I would burn my throat on mine, taking little sips that made the back of my mouth go numb after a while.

When they wanted to start their private talk, Dad would say why didn't we go and play together. They would shut the door behind us.

Tomasz and I used to sit in the hall outside the kitchen. It was a dark hall with a high window at one end. There were bookshelves all the way along the wall with titles in funny letters. (Irena's husband was a professor of Russian literature, so they must have been Russian letters.) The whole house smelt of chicken soup. The carpet was deep green with hundreds and hundreds of brown swirls. I thought I would count them all up one day.

I remember once we were sitting in the hall and it sounded like all the tea things had fallen on the floor. Tomasz looked at me with his watery eyes and we heard Irena make this odd crying sound like someone had hurt her. We just sat there. Tomasz wouldn't touch my toys and I wouldn't touch his. If I did, by accident, I had to scrape the skin where it had touched until it had gone red.

It always felt like there was no one watching, nobody to say what was right or wrong.

The night Tom and his family were coming for dinner, I sat on my parents' bed watching my mother get ready. Tom's cousin and his wife had moved in with them – they needed a place at the moment and they could see Tom's mother through the first patch of being without her husband. The four of them were coming that night.

'I just hope no one's vegetarian,' my mother said. 'I've got so old Andrea won't *rec*ognise me.'

'Why are you so nervous, Mum?'

'I'm not, darling. I think I might be getting a cold.'

When the doorbell rang, I answered. It was strange to see Tom being the son. He looked shorter and younger, standing beside his mother on the doorstep. She was fatter than I expected. I had expected tall, thin, long arms, angular, modern jewellery. She was wearing a long, Indian-looking skirt and a shawl. Hippyish – in a kind of reliving her youth way, I thought. She kissed me hello and said:

'Oh, you tiny thing! You're so tiny I could snap you in half!' She hugged me very hard.

'Simon's just parking the car,' Tom said. 'I'm afraid Rachel couldn't make it because she's feeling shit – so it's just the three of us.'

My mother came up behind and Tom's mother put her arms out. My mother looked embarrassed – she's one of those people who always goes the wrong way, bangs noses, gets people full on the lips. Her dad had a notorious right hook and she is at her best a foot away from people. I watched her move forward, lift her arms and go through with it, saying: 'Andrea, really good to see you again.'

'Jane, Jane,' Andrea sighed. 'Well, we're both a lot older – but that's the one thing we knew would happen.' She laughed and pushed her hair behind her shoulders as if she was rolling up her sleeves.

We were settling down in the sitting room with my father handing out glasses of wine when the doorbell rang.

'Those *fu*cking refugees again,' my dad said, slamming down the bottle of wine.

'No, John, it's my nephew Simon. I'll get it.' Andrea walked out to the door and opened it as if it was her own – I watched my mother's tight face. We listened to them in the hall, kissing each other hello as if they hadn't seen each other for a long time. Tom leant right back in his chair and stuck his legs out, crossed on the carpet.

Andrea walked in behind him with her hand on his shoulder.

'So, this is Simon,' she said. My father was staring at him. I looked at my mother and saw her eyes move over to check

Dad's face. Simon smiled and put his hand out to Mum and then to Dad.

'Don't worry – everyone thinks it,' he said.

'It's ex*traord*inary,' Dad said. He looked almost frightened. I watched Mum glance curiously at Andrea and then she turned her face down at her hands. Simon smiled at me.

'I'm the spitting image of my Uncle Tony – Tom's Dad. People always say it.' He shrugged. Andrea laughed and rubbed Simon's arm. She seemed very proud of him.

'It is amazing, isn't it?'

'Christ, it's as if he'd just gone out for a minute, not twenty years – or whatever it is.'

'It's twenty years, John,' Andrea said.

There was a pause and then my mother laughed the way she does when Dad makes rude jokes in front of Mrs Benton, from the church.

'Oh honestly,' she said, 'poor Simon. Look at all of us. Do sit down and have a drink.'

He smiled and took a big handful of the crisps, which we had all left untouched on the table. I liked the way he had laughed off his big drum roll without seeming embarrassed or secretly proud. Andrea winked at him and he smiled back, indulgently, shaking his head.

Dad and Andrea started a conversation about the book Dad is writing at the moment. I could hear Simon telling my mother about his wife, about her being a costume designer; I heard the words 'incredible things out of nothing' and I could tell he was saying how wonderful she was. 'What a wonderful thing to do,' I heard my mother say. 'She must be wonderful.' Tom was pulling a loose thread out of the cushion beside him and I watched him wind it around his thumb. Every so often he would laugh along with Andrea at something my father was saying, but I didn't think he was listening.

'Well, I do hope she feels better soon,' my mother said, 'poor thing.' The note of gloom in her voice caught Dad's attention and he broke off his story – he loves a disaster.

'Who's that?' he called across. 'What's the matter?'

She spoke slowly, enunciating carefully, the way people do with the very old or the very young,

'It's *Ra*chel, darling – *Si*mon's wife? *Very sad*. She couldn't come tonight because she's got a *mi-graine*.' She often speaks this way to him and he plays up for her in return like a toddler or a bitter old man.

'*Ho*rrible,' Dad said. He screwed his face up.

'Oh, no please don't worry,' Simon told him. He sat forward in his seat. 'I'm sure she'll be fine by tomorrow.' He looked uncomfortable – nervous for a second, and I wondered if there was nothing wrong with her at all and they'd just had a row. My mother changed the subject.

Our sitting room is a big, sunny room. We don't use it often, so the carpet always has the marks of the Hoover across it. The window at one end looks out on to the main road and it's peaceful in there at night with the cars rushing by in waves, saying 'Ssshh' through the double-glazing. Just then the whole room was full of sun. There was a wide patch of light on the carpet almost too bright to look at, except if your eyes moved on the leaf shadows from the tree outside the window. If you watched the leaves, it was like a magic sea.

'So, what do you do, Emily?' Simon asked me. He looked

comfortable again, at ease leaning back against the cushions. This time I took his appearance in. He was elegant, sandy haired, long-limbed. His pale shirt was very bright against his tan and his smile was clean and unaffected. I said I was going to start university soon. He looked surprised.

'Really? I thought – I just assumed you were older than that. What subject?' I told him history. 'Same as me.' He smiled at me and then we both laughed. I don't know why we laughed – we were just laughing. I saw Tom look over.

When I remember that moment now, it seems to have been thrown in so casually. But that's the way things seem to happen to me – the past hinged to the future on a laugh.

'What kind of trees are they down this road?' Simon asked my mother. He turned and looked out of the big window.

'Lime, I think. It's awful, I probably haven't looked at them in years.'

The three of us stared hard out of the window as if that street was the most amazing thing we had ever seen. My mother and I are no good at small talk – she would rather be far away, and I would rather be much closer.

'Very important to have trees if you live in London,' Simon said. 'I said that to Andrea as soon as I saw the place.' He took out a packet of cigarettes. 'Is it all right to smoke in here?'

'Yes, of course. I'll get you an ashtray.'

'Don't worry, I'll get it,' I said.

The health in the tanned face, the crisp shirt, the arm draped over the edge of the sofa – it all suggested he was on good terms with the world. I thought my thin, tense figure must show me up. I wanted to get away for a moment and brush my hair. I went downstairs to the kitchen and leant my hands on the cool sideboard. After a minute or two I heard footsteps on the stairs.

'Hey?' Tom said.

'Hey. Just getting an ashtray for Simon.' I took my hands off that lovely cool marble and turned around.

'I know what you're doing – I was there.'

I started looking around in one of our cupboards. My mother piles the cups one on top of the other in tall, crazy stacks and I am always frightened of knocking them on to the floor – I picture it every time I open the door.

Tom was watching. He came up behind me and put his arms around my waist the way he liked to. He kissed my neck. I could feel the heat of him coming through his shirt.

'This'll do, won't it?' I said. I tilted my head like I was thinking hard, looking at the little blue bowl in my hand. 'Hey, *Tom* – I can't turn round with you like this.' He didn't move and I gave a nervous laugh. My T-shirt had twisted round tight against his arm.

'Tom? Come on, let's get back up there.' I pulled his fingers apart and ducked underneath his arm. I wished he hadn't followed me.

'The loo through there?' he said. I nodded. Then I listened to the floorboards creaking above us – my mother taking the crisps around. I imagined Dad's hand going blindly for the bowl; his face, his whole body turned away from her, into his conversation. He sends her these little messages and I always thought she got each one. I suppose it's something I wish *I* didn't notice.

Tom smiled and pulled me towards him by my belt buckle. He always knew when he could do whatever he wanted. That was our kind of intimacy, I suppose – seeing weakness, knowing how to become indispensable to it. We cured loneliness with sex, dimly aware the problem only became greater and greater, the resentment more intense. His mouth ran across my cheek and down my neck and I closed my eyes, missed a beat. I felt the heat come into my face. My hand was inside his shirt. I felt the smooth muscles in his stomach. Then Tom moved back a little.

'See you up there, then,' he said. He kissed me and then he let go of me, smiling with one side of his mouth.

I picked up the little bowl and walked up the stairs. I felt full of the longing he always brought out in me and I wished it was the middle of the night and we were drunk, dizzy, stumbling into a side street together. My face looked flushed in the hall mirror, my hair looked tangled. Oh, so what, I thought. I went back in.

Before we all went down to eat, Mum laid the table in the kitchen. It was lovely to walk down seeing the knives and forks shining on the white cloth and to smell the pastry and onions cooking. Andrea's heels clacked around the stone floor, she ran her fingers over things.

'My God, this brings back *so* much,' she said. 'It's different now, of course, but you don't forget the *shape* of a room, the *feel* of it, do you?' She made a gasping sound, widened her eyes. 'Wait a minute, though, isn't that our bedroom through there?'

'Yes it's a – it's a little sitting room now,' my mother said. She was walking through quickly, switching lights on so Andrea could see. They went through. The room felt quiet without Andrea – but more peaceful. There are some people who carry a whole fairground of emotions with them wherever they go.

Simon looked at my father, smiling –

'Such a shame you all lost touch.'

Dad smiled. He tore the foil off the red wine, unwinding it in a practised curl.

'Ah well, Tony and Andrea were always destined for more exciting things, Simon. Jane and I would never have kept up.'

Dad likes to tread this line between insult and injury – he likes to watch the nerves on other people's faces. But Simon responded simply,

'Oh, no, they're not like that. They don't drop people.'

Dad came over with the bottle and handed Simon a new glass. There was a kind of amused respect on his face as he filled it.

'Well, things drift – people drift as you get older. You'll find that,' he said.

'Maybe. I hope not.'

I could see Simon did not much like my father.

When they came back in, Andrea sat down heavily at the table.

'Twenty-six,' she said. 'That's how old we were, would you believe it? I can't believe I was twenty-six – ever. I went from baby to old lady like *that* –' she snapped her fingers and laughed a bit wildly. Her nails were bright pink. 'Oh poor decrepit me. But really – *twenty-six*.' She shook her head. I like people who laugh at what they say and then say it again more seriously. Andrea pulled her shawl off and then swung it around herself again so that the tassels spun out and slapped down against her back. Simon handed her a glass of wine. He was attentive to her and she took obvious – almost flirtatious – pleasure in it.

'What were *we* like at twenty-six, darling?' Dad said.

My mother was laying out melon and prosciutto for everyone. She had arranged it prettily with the meat in little curls. She put a plate in front of me.

'What? I don't know,' she said. 'We're the same people, I suppose. Aren't we? I really don't remember thinking very differently then.'

'Oh, *Jane* – you must believe in a lot of different things now, though,' Andrea said. 'I mean, you've had children; you've lost your parents. Think of all the things you didn't understand then. I sometimes think getting older is about every year of your life understanding another terrible thing people do. You start out thinking "I will never do a job I don't like, the way some idiots do" and then gradually, gradually, you begin to understand divorce, alcoholism, violence – even murder. You can put yourself in a lot of unexpected places by the end of it.'

'No. I've always known what I believe in – I've known my whole life.'

I also like people who do not laugh at what they say. I watched my mother as she walked over to the oven and checked the timer. There was a tension between her and Andrea which seemed to have been summed up in their exchange. They were summing themselves up for each other the way people do who haven't met for a long time.

'Wow, you're a lucky man, John – if you've still got the girl you married,' Andrea said. She laughed, 'Seriously.'

'*Aren't* I?' my dad said. But Andrea was not really listening,

'God, I'm completely different – and look what's happened to me.' She waved her naked ring finger, the skin still paler where the ring had been for all those years. 'The problem with my formula is for every inch you gain of understanding, you lose two of idealism. You end up having more time for the face on the "Have-you-seen-this-man" poster than you do for your own husband.'

She looked from Mum to Dad and then back to Mum again, smiling. I wondered if this dinner had been a good idea.

'But sometimes people both change the same way, don't they? It doesn't have to end in – that.' Simon looked at Andrea's ring hand as if she shouldn't have brought it out in front of people. She smiled at him and squeezed his arm.

'Oh, of course it doesn't, Simon. Some people are too good and loving for life to be hard on them.' There was an innocence in his face which she responded to, which we all responded to. Andrea looked relieved to drop her hard, bright manner and watch him, sentimentally.

'Seriously, though,' he said. 'I mean, I used to say, "You only know you were in love in retrospect." How bleak can you get? You only know you were in love when you've had time to rewrite it, time to edit the script – and for God's sake don't call the girl and find she isn't in character. All that crap. And then I met Rachel and there was that whole thing with her going into hospital –' he looked up and waved the details off with his hand, 'and I knew love wasn't about *re*trospect or pre*dic*tions or any kind of thinking at all. I just sat by her bed.'

'Oh, Simon,' Andrea said.

'You just have to put the other person before yourself,

don't you? Isn't that what you have to do? I mean, I'm twenty-six – exactly the same age as you and Uncle Tony were when you lived in that room – I don't want to think the same thing is going to happen to me.'

I dug my nails into my hand.

'I really don't think it has to,' I said. Sometimes, by chance, you see your very own mixture of hope and fear on a stranger's face. It feels like a miracle of intimacy – as if it was built outside of time, independently of the details of two different lives. He looked at me and smiled as if I was his old friend. His smile was a cool hand and I felt my face relax.

'Exactly,' he said – as if it was proof enough that I agreed with him. I could feel his eyes rest on me.

Andrea laughed.

'You're not going to begrudge me my new start, I hope – you two puritans?'

Her voice seemed to shock Simon out of his thoughts. He looked at her with real tenderness on his face.

'Andrea, I'm going to make that place fantastic for you – wait and see.'

When they left, Tom said he was going to stay for a while; he told them he would get a cab home later. My parents said good night and went up to bed.

'You can't stay the night,' I told him. 'My mother would go mad.'

'She's sweet,' he said.

'I'm glad you like her.'

'Yeah – she's a proper mother. Look, I won't stay long, let's just have a coffee.'

I made the coffee and he sat at the kitchen table, smoking a cigarette and finishing the wine.

'Thank you,' he said, when I put the cup down in front of him. It felt very late, even though we were usually together long past that time. I suppose it was because we were sober.

'D'you get on with Andrea?' I asked him.

'She's my mother.'

'You're quite different, that's all. What about your Dad?'

'Dad's amazing. I just don't get to see him that much.'

He did not seem to want to talk. He sat at the table, holding the cup in his crazy hands, all the nails bitten right down. His beautiful face was completely passive, as if he was all on his own. You are on your own with me, I thought – I felt useless to him. I watched him drink his coffee. The dishwasher was loud in the background.

Chapter two

Tom and I had fun together. We stayed out all night and came home drunk in the fragile, blue time. London was as full of contradictions as we were: all brazen lights towards night and shamefaced street corners at dawn. Whatever state he was in, Tom always wanted to drive me back. We would drive along the river, in the still air, past the warehouses and the amazing, high, glass offices. It was still hot at five, six in the morning and I would hang my arm out of the window while we drove. We always had sex in the car before I went in. When I put my key in the lock, it felt hot and secret under the low-down sky.

I loved having sex with Tom. When I look back now, I can hardly understand who I was then. But it was me – my hands, my hips, my legs – and I loved it.

We drove around a lot. The driving was the best part. There

would be four of Tom's friends in the back seat of his car – maybe Jay, Andrew, Nick and Ronnie – and we would go and eat and then decide where to go for the night. Whatever we decided, someone was always sure there was a better party somewhere else. There were funny arguments. People's mobiles were always going, people were always looking for lighters, wanting to change the song. We played music loud and felt young at the traffic lights.

A lot of nights we went to bars and clubs. They were places I had never heard of and I knew Tom liked that. His favourite place only got started at 3 a.m. It was called 'Raf's' . It had a broken, pink neon sign outside it. The sign flickered on and off and made a threatening, electrical noise like a rattlesnake – it made you look up from time to time when you were in the queue. Everybody was older than us in there. Their clothes were beautiful. I loved watching. By the end of the night, the glasses knocking together and the perfect laughter were like blinding camera flashes, every time.

I used to go up on to the street for air sometimes and I made friends with the bouncer. His name was Grenville. He was six foot three with short dreadlocks which stuck up like baby snakes all over his head. He told me stories about fights and his shadow would look like a madcap cartoon character leaping around on the pavement in front of us. He told me how the manager had said to flirt with the little rich girls when they came in – girls like me, but not like me, he said.

'Some of these girls were grown in orchid houses,' the manager had told him. He told him having a big, black man kiss them on the cheek, Continental style, would give them a little thrill. Grenville laughed.

'You got big money coming from little thrills,' he said.

'Charlotte baby', 'Laura baby' I heard him call them – it sounded funny and it was all a careful lie, just like a broken neon sign where five drinks would pay to fix it.

I had only had glimpses of this fashionable side of London before. It was all too expensive for me, and in the past I had tried not to look beyond the round of smoky gatherings at my friends' houses. When we left school, though, most of my friends went straight to university. I backpacked for four months, around Italy and Spain, where my mother has various relations. When I came home, all the routines of my old social life had gone. For a few weeks there was a soft formlessness to my life. I felt like a child again, I hung around the house watching TV with my little sister. The books I was meant to be reading for university sat unnoticed on the hall table, belonging to another life. Then Sarah, who had been in the year below me at school, threw a party.

That was when I met Tom – and after that, his friends. I liked having a new set of people to spend time with. They were glossier than my old friends, more worldly, funded by larger allowances. I was accepted without question, because I was with Tom.

I would look at him sometimes, while we waited by the bar or when we sat down at a table, and wonder what he thought about – what he was going to do with his life. I had heard him say something about being a film producer once – get into his dad's world, he said. His distant tone of voice made me think about those books of mine unread on the hall table. For a moment I felt sad and a little bit frightened. Ronnie laughed.

'Shit, yeah – Tom, you could produce or whatever, Jay could be the director and I could be like your leading man. Awesome – we'll make a packet.'

'Exactly, man,' Tom said, but again distantly – as if he was talking about someone else.

Mostly he just talked about what he would do the next night. From time to time he would look back at me in the bar and hold my gaze. It was like he was holding my eyes down, saying 'This is what you get: eyes.' Just eyes. Maybe he was just looking at me and thinking about the time in the car the night before. I suppose there was a kind of privacy in not being known at all.

'You OK, Em? Happy?' – Too loud to hear the words – I watched his mouth. He would hand me his wallet and I'd go off to the loos and have a line.

And I was happy – or at least I was excited all the time I was with him. Tom was so good looking people watched him whatever he was doing. I watched him – his arm resting on the bar, the muscles through his T-shirt when he reached over for his drink. Lust was like a spotlight trained on me sometimes and I loved it. I felt famous. The music was amazing at that place and we danced for hours.

Some nights we stopped off at a little casino that was owned by Nick's dad. Mr Giorgiou used to come down to say hello. He didn't want Nick gambling, but he didn't mind if we had some fun.

'Have some fun, kids,' he would say. Tom hated him, he said Mr Giorgiou used to feel up his leg when he was little, when he went to Nick's house to swim in their pool. You could picture the big hands.

The casino was small; not in an exclusive way – in a small way. It looked and felt like the end of something there. Just the night, maybe – I always over-react. It was just the peeling wallpaper and the disinfectant smell from the loos. I don't really know why we went there – probably Tom just did it to make Nick feel good about himself. His friends relied on him for that. He always said they were too good for the girls they were with: 'You're the *Man,* Jay – don't even let her *trouble* you,' and I knew Ronnie and Jay borrowed money from him.

None of us had enough for gambling, but it was exciting to watch the people who did. One time we watched a man lose £2,000 playing blackjack. His lips went white. It was a lot of money for that place and the dealer put his hand on the man's shoulder and glanced around to see if there was anyone with him. For a moment I wished I could pretend. What did I think I could do? Take him home, make a hot drink, tuck him up?

He wasn't with anyone. We watched him take a few tries to get himself up. It was too private to watch him walk out of the room.

'*Total* dickhead,' Tom whispered in my ear. Now I realise how often he shocked me.

'Total.' 'Totally.' That word came up again and again in his speech. He was a mathematician in life, adding up circumstances, characteristics until he got one – a total – and made his judgement. He was only interested in absolutes, the way his fingers were only happy when the chip of paint came off whole.

Then we would be off driving again. We drove everywhere

– even when it would have been quicker to walk. We sat in traffic for ages, but it really was exciting to be there under the lights in Piccadilly Circus or Trafalgar Square, smoking and laughing in Tom's car. All the radio stations were designed for us.

Some nights we went to parties – going in was the best moment – the way the music came ballooning into you and the way girls looked at Tom. His friends joked about it and I would laugh. I laughed hard because I knew he only wanted me – it doesn't make me proud to remember that now. But there is a lot of safety in being envied – even if you know the real worth of what you have. Sometimes I lived for whole evenings in other girls' jealous fantasies. I watched them envying me in the corner of my eye and laughed secretly when they twitched their faces away.

One guy, Ed, had a party at his house almost every night. He was an actor, who had been in a popular sitcom when he was thirteen. Tom said: 'Eddie used to be really good looking and now he has it all on video.' He was only twenty-eight, but he had turned out a lot narrower and longer faced than they had expected. He had only done a few adverts since – he told me about it himself: boy eating Fish Dippas, boy with dirty T-shirt puts it in washing machine. He had sad eyes and the loudest laugh I have ever heard. His flat was amazing, all whitewash and aluminium and candles. The bottom two flats in the building were empty and dark, and with the lights and music falling out of his windows – it looked like they had been suffocated by the bouncing, hyperactive child above.

If you climbed out of Ed's bedroom window, you could get on to the roof. There was a flat rectangle of tarmac and then the roof sloped down right over the road. A few of us were sitting up there one night, when Ed had an argument with his girlfriend. It was very late – the end of a night – and we were all drunk.

'Oh fuck yourself,' she told him. These were the kind of statements she made.

'Save me a lot of money if I could, wouldn't it?' he said.

We were all looking now. She grabbed his wallet out of his jeans and threw it out across the roof. It skidded and slid right to the edge, by the guttering.

'What the fuck'd you do that for?' he shouted. Kate was standing up, tying back her hair, getting ready to go back down. She was laughing. She had sparkly, red shoes on and I watched the way she pushed her left foot in and out of one of them, while she waited to see what Ed would do.

'All my fucking *cards* are in there, Kate. You *know* that.' A crackle of hysteria ran through the air.

Tom's voice was so smooth it made us all look round.

'I'll get it,' he said.

'No, man – don't be stupid, you'll fall off. You'll kill yourself. *Jesus*, Kate, there's eighty quid in there.'

'Money, money, *money*,' Kate said – she leant right in at his face. She had started crying and she climbed back down through Ed's window. He stood still for a moment, looking down into the road. A motorbike shot past leaving sound behind it.

'Fuck it,' he said. 'I'd better go and see if she's OK.'

'Look, I'll go,' Tom said. 'Sometimes it's better if it's someone else.'

When he had gone, Ed sat down and lit a cigarette. He

could look really tired sometimes. No one could think of anything to say and you could hear people's cigarettes burning when they took a drag. I looked at the cloud of light around the street lamp and thought about sleep.

After a few minutes, we heard Kate's voice saying: 'What? Why is this your business, Tom?'

They went on talking, but you could only hear Kate; Tom must have been using the quiet, smooth voice.

Soon they both climbed out of the window. Tom was holding Kate's wrist and you could hear her breathing in little snatches of air. Her hair was hanging in her face. They walked out in front of us and then Kate started to edge her way down the roof towards the wallet. She leant on one hand and sloped her body diagonally against the tiles. You could hear her crying – she was drunk and scared. She looked like a thin, stray cat and you could see the cars below, snaking in the gaps between her bony arms and legs. I think we all suddenly realised how drunk we were, because people started straightening themselves up.

Ed looked at me. He mouthed 'What the fuck?' and gestured at Tom. I stood up, but I did not know what to do. The truth is I was always scared of disagreeing with Tom – even about where to go for the night. If you questioned his judgement, he was humiliated. And his embarrassment was more potent than other people's. He had a way of stabbing you with his eyes to stop you looking, to shut you up.

'K*a*tie,' Ed shouted out. 'Get back up here. This is *dangerous*. Come back up here.' He stood up and the wine bottle next to him tipped over and rolled away a little. 'Listen, sweetie, it doesn't matter – we'll get it tomorrow. I'll hook it up with a broom or something tomorrow. Katie?' He looked at Tom. 'What the fuck, Tom?'

'What?'

'What have you said to her?'

'Nothing. Look, you're really good to her, Ed. You buy dinner almost every night, you get her clothes, you take her on holiday. What does she think is going on?'

'That's just money,' Ed said. 'It's just my dad's money for fuck's sake, Tom. I *love* her. I love you, Katie. Come back up.'

'She's cold, Ed. She's making a total fool of you.'

Ed looked at Tom like he didn't recognise him and then he went after Katie and helped her back up the roof. They started kissing each other when they got to the top and then Ed said we should all call it a night.

'Katie is neurotic,' Tom told me on the way home. I remember the way his cheeks hollowed on the last of his cigarette and then he turned and said it to me. I can see the flash of his pale face in the street light, like a fish turning in dark water.

'Total.' 'Totally.' Now I think there was nothing that added up to anything in our times together. They were all broken – broken sentences, forgotten names, spilt drinks – blackouts. Nothing good could come out of so much broken, lost stuff. 'I love you,' Tom said – and he got my mouth. Just my mouth. There was an absolute for him. Did I really imagine he didn't notice?

I knew he had seen a lot of girls before he started going out with me. They used to call him on his mobile, their names would flash up on the little screen – 'Jen', 'Sarah', 'Lucy', 'Emily' – some other Emily for me to wonder about. He would brush them off quickly, saying:

'Uh-huh. Yeah? Well, I might be there. Maybe,' until they dropped it – whatever it was. If they were around, his friends would want to know who had called for that kind of treatment. Once, when Tom answered 'Jessie', they all laughed hard in the back of the car. Nick made a clicking noise with his tongue and ruffled Tom's hair. Ronnie said: 'You have got it *bad*, my friend.'

About two weeks after Simon and Andrea came for dinner, my parents went away to visit a friend of Dad's. I had mentioned it to Tom and he turned up the afternoon they went. He had dropped me off at five that morning and I had only just got up and read the note my mum had left about food and the gas man and looking after my little sister. Ellie was still in bed and I was having a cup of coffee on my own in the kitchen when the doorbell went. He was wearing last night's clothes and he said he needed a coffee – if I didn't mind giving him a cup of coffee, he said. He was angry about something.

'Of course you can have a coffee,' I told him. We went down to the kitchen.

'So, where did you go,' I asked him, 'afterwards?'

'Afterwards?'

'After you – said goodbye to me.'

'Oh, after I said "*goodbye*".' He winced at my primness, but he couldn't have referred to the fact that we'd had sex in his car any more than I could. He looked away and affected a yawn. A childish anger that this was not how things were meant to be between men and women made my cheeks feel hot. 'I went on to Ed's,' he told me.

'You should look after yourself, Tom.'

'You think so?'

'Yes, I think so.' He stank of alcohol and smoke. 'Would you like a bath?'

'Not clean enough for you, am I? Do I stink?'

'Jesus, Tom – I just thought you might like a bath.'

He straightened his shirt and pushed his hair back.

'Look, I'm sorry, Em. I'm just tired. Come and give me a kiss.'

I didn't want to, with that smell on him, but I did so we wouldn't have to have an argument.

I only opened my eyes when I heard my little sister coming down the stairs.

'It's Ellie,' I said. I pulled Tom's hand away from my leg and started clanking coffee cups around on the other side of the kitchen, thinking how like Mum I am after all.

'Hi,' Ellie said. Her hair was in a mess and she pulled at the hem of her T-shirt to make it longer on her bare legs. She glanced at Tom and said: 'Has Mum gone?'

'They went hours ago. D'you want hot chocolate?'

'Yes please.'

She sat down at the table near Tom.

'I'm Tom – nice to meet you.' He put his hand out to her like a businessman and she giggled and shook it.

'How d'you do – I'm Eloise.'

'I know. I've heard about you.'

Her eyes flashed at me.

'Just that you're my lovely little sister,' I said. I gave her the hot chocolate and remembered a time when my friend and I had put a sign on my bedroom door saying: 'No Entry If You Are Called Ellie and You Smell'.

'You don't look like each other,' Tom said.

'Not much, no.'

When I was pouring the coffee I heard Ellie whisper:

'My sister's really beautiful.'

'So are you,' Tom whispered back.

I put the pot of coffee down in front of them.

'Any chance of some toast?'

'I'll do it – can I?' Ellie said.

I drank my coffee and watched her slicing the bread and getting out the jam and the honey and the butter. She looked over at him anxiously.

'We've got Marmite, too.'

'Honey,' he said. 'I like honey.'

'Me too. It's *my* favourite, too.' She got a spoon for it, which is what Mum does even though we always use our knives anyway. She buttered the toast for him and put it down on the table. 'I'll give you the jam *just in case*,' she said. She looked happy getting things for him and I looked out of the window, into the garden, for a while. There was sun on the orange blossom and the wind went through the grass.

It made me feel peaceful to look out there. I thought I would go for a long walk later, maybe take some of those books with me. Make a start. And I would take a rug and sandwiches and have a delicious picnic all on my own – cheese and French bread and strawberries. And then I would read and fall asleep with the sun on my face. I would keep the peaceful feeling.

I used to be good at peace and quiet. I would walk around the garden barefoot for ages, seeing if I could separate every smell in the air: grass, roses, lunch cooking, the dog next door wet from its bath. Uncle Peter told me to do it – he said it was how to be happy, noticing every little thing and taking pleasure in it. It was one of his peaceful afternoons; sometimes he is loud and sarcastic and drinks as much as Dad. He is the most romantic person I have ever met but he lives alone. I always thought he had nice ideas, though.

Tom's phone went. He took it out of his shirt pocket and looked at it angrily, saying,

'*Definitely* not in.' He pressed a button, 'Zap – you're dead,' and the phone stopped ringing.

'Wow, can I see?' Ellie said.

'Sure.'

She held it carefully.

'This is like about the most expensive phone you can get.'

'Is it?'

The way Tom sat, with one arm resting on the back of his chair, I wondered if maybe this was what he was used to.

'Everyone wants these. There's this girl at school – Helen – who gets to use her Mum's one, sometimes. She's a bitch, though – like most people at my school.' She handed the phone back to him and he looked at it for a second,

'Hey – what've you done to it?'

Ellie laughed the way the child with the snowball does.

'Nothing.'

'This is in Russian or something.'

'Finnish, actually.'

'Change it back, Ellie,' I said.

'He just has to follow the instructions.'

'I can't – they're in Finnish.' She stuck her tongue out at him and giggled. 'You little . . .' He jumped up laughing and chased her round the back of the table. She squealed and, for a moment, I remembered a picnic when Dad had flu and Uncle Peter came instead and we made a raft and pretended the field was a crashing sea. I miss Uncle Peter.

'Ow! Let me go,' Ellie shouted. Tom was tickling her. Her hair was all over her face – you could just see her open mouth through it, pink and laughing, gasping for breath. Her T-shirt had got twisted round and pulled up above her knickers; the pattern on them was little pink pigs, running in all directions. 'Please . . . please . . .' she was saying, through her laughter. His hand moved to her stomach now and her arm knocked the orange juice into the sink – you could hear it glugging down the drain.

'I'm going to tickle you and tickle you until I make you wet yourself,' Tom said.

I jumped up, suddenly desperate to get away.

'Just taking the rubbish out,' I told them. I ran up the stairs and out on to the street. I had tears in my eyes – I did not ask myself why. I saw Tom's car and I flinched at the thought of him that morning – my spine rammed against the steering wheel, the gearstick bruising my leg, his face angry and resolute and the way it had all made me shout out and then shake long afterwards.

'I love you,' he said and I had laughed a little, because it looked so much like its opposite.

'Hi Emily,' someone said. I looked up and it was Simon. 'Hey, you all right?'

'I'm all right,' I said.

'OK. You looked worried for a minute.'

'Worried? No, I'm fine.'

He was eating a sandwich. His hair had blown around in the wind. He was wearing an old blue shirt with holes in the elbows and it made him look young and comfortable. He took a mouthful of his sandwich and pointed with it, over the road –

'Just having a look at the place. There's such a lot of work to be done. I've been over working it all out this morning.' He patted the tape measure in his shirt pocket and grinned as if he was very proud of himself.

I thought about all those empty rooms, the bare walls and the scrubbed, wooden floors. Imagine having a place like that, I thought: having a long bath, feeling clean and simple, walking around barefoot on the floorboards, not telling anyone you were home. It was always a dream of mine – an empty place where no one would think to find you.

'Anyway,' Simon said, 'you're busy.' He looked down at the rubbish bag I was holding and I felt ridiculous for a second. I went through the actions in my mind, the 'bye then – see you soon, I hope', his figure walking away down the road, stuffing the rubbish bag in the dirty, black bin and going back down to the kitchen. I should go back down there, I thought, and look after Ellie.

But I suppose I have always worried about Ellie – and just then I didn't want to.

'Can I see the house? I've never been in,' I said.

He gave me his broad smile.

'Course you can. Want a bite?' he held his sandwich out to me.

'I'm fine – hangover.'

'You should eat more. Out with Tom, were you?'

We walked towards the house. I told myself Ellie would be fine for ten minutes. She would just think I'd gone to the newsagent's. I would apologise – we could do something together that afternoon, I thought. Ellie makes you feel protective. When we were little I used to wish someone would mug us on the way back from school just so I could stand in front of her and say hit me instead, take *my* pocket money. I've become selfish. I've become a bad sister to Ellie and I know it. The strange thing is, I resented it sometimes, but when I stopped caring enough about her, I stopped caring enough about anything.

I looked at Simon and wondered what he thought of me and Tom. Did he roll his eyes, I wondered, and get on with being seriously married?

The front garden was overgrown and there were bin bags full of weeds lined up by the wall. Through the window, you could see little squares of colour – tests – painted on the walls.

'I want to get this whole place sorted out – make it really happy for Andrea,' he said. 'I've got vision, you know: rose bushes, jasmine by the door. Four bin bags down. Who knows?' He shook his head and seemed to be laughing at himself and then he unlocked the front door.

'I love that smell,' I told him.

'Clean and empty,' he said. 'Come and look at this.'

We started to go up the stairs and I wondered why Simon was doing all of this, what Tom was doing for Andrea. His loyalty seemed as unquestioned as Tom's selfishness. We went along the corridor, into the bright room at the end. The bed was still in there. It was a huge double bed, with a wrought-iron frame around it draped in a hysterical amount of muslin. The muslin was pale cream and hung forward in thick, lazy folds where it was tied back with ribbons at each side. It was an amazing bed – but a bit embarrassing to look at, it was so obviously someone's secret dream.

'Isn't it wonderful?' he said. 'Intimidating, though. Imagine the histrionics a bed like this would expect.'

'Tears before bedtime,' I said. We smiled at each other. 'I wonder why they left it.' It was the only thing they had left.

'Some people don't care about things, I suppose. They just buy new stuff.'

I thought about the Lebanese couple. Perhaps they really had split up. Perhaps they had known they could find places for all the other stuff – the glasses, the kitchen table. Not the bed they had shared, though – that would be useless. I wondered what could have happened to them. I didn't want to mention them or how happy they had looked, because it might have stopped Simon smiling at me like that.

'You're a funny one, aren't you?' he said. 'I've never seen a person look like they were feeling so many things at once. I can't work you out, Emily.'

'Oh, don't do that.'

'You're all right – I'm completely useless with women,' he said – and we laughed, because it was plain he wasn't.

I walked towards the doorway and looked along the landing, 'Don't you almost wish it was going to stay like this, though? It feels so peaceful with nothing in it.'

'You should see how much stuff Andrea's got. God knows how we're going to squeeze it in, to be honest. Still, it's twenty-odd years of her life, I suppose – of her memories.'

'Of course it is. I'm being stupid – I just like things simple, that's all.'

He laughed and walked ahead of me back down the stairs again. I felt a pulse of insecurity and wanted to ask him what was so funny. I wished I hadn't said that – about liking things simple – it would sound childish, unrealistic to him. He stopped to examine a crack in the plaster.

'Yeah,' he sighed. 'It is weird how possessions just creep up on you, isn't it? You literally acquire weight through life – every place you go. Rachel and I had box after box of rubbish.'

The adult solidity of their lives was so far beyond me – there seemed no point in pretending.

'Not me – I lose everything. I'd only fill about half a suitcase with everything I own.'

'Really? What does that say about you, I wonder?'

'Oh, I don't know,' I said. For a second I wondered what Rachel was like, if she was beautiful.

'Yeah – maybe just that you're very young.'

We walked around the rest of the house a bit, and I said the right things about high ceilings and light, but I didn't really notice any of it. I felt an intense loneliness, as if his comment about my age was a locked door he had pointed out to me and now I would always feel I was outside it.

It was too hot on the street after those shady rooms. A tepid breeze rattled the bushes beside us. We stopped outside the gate and I wished I had asked more questions about the house, made it all last longer. I felt peaceful in his company.

'D'you know where Tom is at the moment?' he said. 'I tried his mobile about half an hour ago, but it was on voicemail – or

I got politely diverted.' He laughed warmly and I felt ashamed, remembering Tom looking at his phone and saying 'definitely not in'.

'Yeah, he's at my house.'

'Is he? Oh, right. Well, could you say Andrea really wants to hear from him – he just disappears and she goes mad worrying. Just get him to call, would you?' He looked away and his eyes narrowed as if he was trying to make something out right at the end of the road.

'Sure,' I said. I was ashamed of myself and of Tom. I thought we must seem so young and lost to someone like Simon. He checked his watch and sighed.

'Builders are late.'

I tried to shake my head knowingly,

'I promise I'll get Tom to call,' I told him.

Chapter three

'Andrea, this is really kind of you,' I heard my mother saying. I watched her wind the curly lead from the phone around her wrist a few times. 'No, it'll be really lovely. Let's hope this weather holds.'

She paused.

'Well, why don't I ask her – she's right here,' she said. 'Em? Have you got anything planned for Sunday? Andrea's having a lunch party . . .' She held her breath and smiled painfully at the voice in her ear: 'it's a "Farewell to the old house" party.' She raised her eyebrows at me.

'No,' I said, 'I'm around.'

'Emily says she'd love to,' my mother said. 'So that's great. Thank you so much, Andrea. OK then. Yes, OK then. OK then, Andrea. Goodbye.'

She put down the receiver and pulled her hand free of the cord as if she was brushing off something dirty.

'We'll just pop in,' she said. She wrinkled up her nose and shrugged. 'We don't have to stay till the end.'

She walked away towards the washing-up.

'Won't we want to stay till the end?'

'What? Oh, I don't know, Em. Andrea's friends are . . . They're – I don't know. Dad liked them.'

An image of my father laughing, drinking with friends came into my mind. I knew this seemed just as implausible to Mum from the way she turned the taps on full to end the conversation. My father doesn't 'like' – he smiles his crooked smile at people. Just one side of his mouth – he's not going to lift both sides of it for just anybody. He is sometimes amused by people, though. I imagined Andrea's amusing friends – frustrated actors and architects, bored wives of bankers. Dad enjoys bored people. He likes imagining how they got that way – he reconstructs it on the way home, making it sound inevitable.

Just then he walked past the doorway, illustrating himself, the way people do sometimes. I watched his sloped shoulders, the lines on his forehead. He was carrying a paper, a book which the light gleamed off for a moment. His shirt had come untucked at the back. I wished I could think of something to say to him.

Later Tom rang to ask if I was coming.

'You don't have to,' he said. 'It'll be pretty boring.'

'Would you prefer if I didn't?'

'No. Nothing like that. Just that it'll be lots of Mum's crazy old friends and Simon and Rachel going around being perfect.

Just so you know it's not going to be a great party or anything.'

'It's OK,' I said, 'I'll come.'

'Fine.'

I really didn't care that he didn't want me to come. I imagined some stupid self-consciousness about his room or the way his mother's friends still ruffled his hair and it didn't seem serious enough to care about.

My mother thinks I don't take anything that seriously. She mentioned this to the family counsellor once. (We only went three times – it was when Ellie started saying she didn't want supper and Mum found crisp packets in her room. I'm amazed we went at all. The last time Dad had a row with her about Jung.) This was the second time we went. My mother glanced at me sideways, as if it was a betrayal, and then she said:

'It's as though she's bored. It's no way to live. You can't go on like that – with nothing mattering.'

'Course you can,' my dad said. 'We've got a frivolous gene. She's her father's daughter, Jane. Emily looks at life with a wry smile.'

'I don't see her smiling, John,' my mother said. 'Or you.'

The day of Andrea's lunch party was beautiful. It was the kind of day which makes you feel you're breathing in the sunlight with the air. I could smell the orange blossom in the garden through my bedroom window. I put on my white dress.

Dad was too busy working to come and Ellie was staying with a friend. Mum and I drove over there together, both of us wondering what Andrea was leaving behind. The heat made patches of air ripple above the road.

By the time we got there, the laughing and talk were

already splashing out on to the street. The garden surrounded the house. There were tall hedges in front and you could just see the house through the leaves, sitting like an island fortress in the middle. Tom had told me his parents had a thing about privacy. He said you had to drive to their last place – in France – through a small wood, so in comparison this place felt buzzing. He rolled his eyes. Even I could already see Andrea was someone who needed attention, gossip. They had averaged just two years at each place. They must have gone quiet with a thud after all the builders, the removal men had gone.

But Andrea was a person who set herself tests. I wondered how she felt about moving back to the street where she and Tony started out – alone now. Tony had moved abroad, bought another secluded dream with another woman, apparently. Andrea's new house had a front lawn which made it feel wide open to the street, it had next-door houses close by on either side. Perhaps for her, at least, the loop of years had been a process of emergence.

My mother locked the car door and smiled at me. There were coins of sunlight on her hair.

'Sounds like a lot of people,' she said. 'We don't have to stay till the end.'

We walked through the gate with our bottle of wine. I could hear Tom's voice: 'Where? On the sideboard, Mum? Are they on the sideboard?' but he must have gone inside before we reached the main part of the garden.

Andrea saw us straight away. She had a straw sun hat on and a long, yellow dress. There were heavy, silver bracelets on her arms. She touched the hand of the person she was talking to and put on a new smile for us.

'So *glad*,' she called out, '*love*ly you could make it.' She walked towards us with her arms out.

'Andrea, this is all fantastic,' my mother said. 'I feel completely underdressed.'

'Don't be silly, Jane – you're your lovely self. Oh, Emily you look so pretty.' She turned me round as if she had made my dress herself. 'Tom's just inside. Shall I run and get him – or will you survive for a moment?'

'I'm fine,' I said.

'You look *so* pretty – wait till he sees you. You're a little spirit – a nymph. Beautiful,' she said. I wanted her to stop. She looked from side to side and then moved closer as though she was going to tell us a secret.

'Listen, I'll let you in on it, but you mustn't say a *word* to Tom. Promise?'

My mother was red in the face. She looked down at her bottle of wine.

'Of course, Andrea,' she said.

'Well, it's not definite, because love him as we do, we all know Tony's an unreliable bastard, but he's in London for the weekend and he's said he'll drop by. Tom'll be *thrilled* if he does, but I don't want to get his hopes up, if you know what I mean. He gets so hurt. He's so *sensitive*.' She looked right at me. 'You must know, Emily, how sensitive Tom is.'

I nodded.

'Look, there he is. Mum's the word. To-om?' she sang out.

It took him a moment to trace her voice. People's voices seemed to get lost in Andrea's garden the way they do at the seaside, in all the water and distance. He came across the lawn holding a tray of wine glasses.

'You could have put those down, darling,' Andrea said. She laughed and stroked his hair. Tom put the tray on the grass and leant over awkwardly to kiss me on both cheeks.

'Hello, Jane,' he said to my mother. I wondered if she suspected we slept together. There was a pause and then Andrea filled it with her laugh and her bracelets.

'Aren't you going to get Emily a drink, Tom? Honestly,' she said. She raised her eyes. 'Jane, you come with me and we'll leave these two to the anxieties of love and youth. Thank *God* we've done all that stuff.'

Andrea's clipped, jaunty way of talking seemed designed to draw attention to her sadness, rather than to hide it. She knew it made a poignant contrast with that weary look in her eyes. She took my mother's arm – as if she really was as old and tired as she suggested – and they walked away across the grass.

I looked out after them. Andrea's friends were standing around in small groups, laughing and talking. They wore linen jackets, long dresses – the more theatrical women wore patterned sarongs; the wind blew them full like sails. It was a beautiful garden, luscious and multicoloured, just beginning to crack and curl in the heat. For a moment, the shady canopy of a large, dark tree moved over. Suddenly, the sunlight filled out the glasses of wine and they glinted wildly and threw coloured shadows – fragments of stained-glass windows – on to white shirts and pale arms. I felt incredibly happy to be seeing it all. The music from the house got rushed away in the wind along with the laughter and the talking, then back they came – like excited children who had been too far out.

'Black or white?' Tom said. I must have stared at him. 'Wine? D'you want red or white?'

We went to the long table to get a drink and then sat down on the step into the kitchen. It was good to be out of the sun.

'Lots of people,' I said. I drank some of the wine and smiled, thinking how different we were. I wondered what Tom would think of me if he knew that when I was fourteen I used to say spells for true love, that I used to light candles and sprinkle rosewater, sleep on my right side because someone said you dreamt of your husband that way. I bit my lip to stop the smile and looked at him.

'Yeah, it's a good turnout,' Tom said.

'Are any of your friends coming?'

'Maybe later.' He looked down at his hands, which were pulling at mint leaves from the little bush by the door. I thought perhaps it had been a mistake to come – that we wouldn't know how to behave without his friends and all the drinks and the music. His sigh was like a pressure valve.

'Look, I'm sorry I've been weird recently,' he told me.

I looked away, not knowing what I should say to him. I hate any kind of confession.

'I know I've been weird,' he said again. 'I'm sorry, OK?'

'Sure – it's fine, Tom. Don't worry about it.'

I wondered what he had in mind, because he could have meant so many things: the way he had frightened Katie on Ed's roof, the way he spoke to me when he turned up at my house that morning?

He threw the handful of mint into the garden and laughed. There was a sweet smell.

'Do you even think I have been weird, Em?'

'What?' I said. 'Tom, you and I get on well. Don't you think?'

He laughed softly, leaning his head back against the wall. I looked at his beautiful face and wished I loved him. Sometimes you can imagine how simple things could be. Then he put his hand on my leg, stretching his fingers over my knee, so that it fitted into the palm of his hand –

'Yeah, we get on well,' he said. He pulled my head towards him and locked it in the crook of his arm, the way brothers do sometimes. I liked his playfighting and we laughed together genuinely for the first time in a while – probably since he said he loved me.

'What's the matter with me, Em? I don't know – I'm just . . . forget it.'

He let go of me and I watched the mint leaves roll away in the wind.

'Sure,' I said. 'It's forgotten.' I stroked his hair and then I remembered that was what Andrea did. He had a strange, private expression on and I wanted to look away. I think I did not want to know too much about him.

Simon and Rachel were standing by the big tree, talking to an old lady and a young man, who had his hand on her back. I knew it was Rachel straight away. She had long, brown hair and a tanned face. She was thin and neat looking, almost as tall as Simon. You could see she was pretty even at that distance; there was a balance to her features which made it a mathematical certainty. She had a silver necklace on and the light slid over it every time she turned and looked up at Simon and laughed. She did this often – and who can blame her, I thought. They did look perfect, like Tom said – a tall, straight-backed couple with the sunlight winking off the leaves around them like confetti.

Then I saw Simon notice us. He said something to Rachel and she looked over, narrowing her eyes where he pointed. She smiled and waved.

'Shall we go over?' I said to Tom. But Simon was already walking towards us.

'Look, I should see if I can help out with the food or something. Simon'll look after you – he's very good socially,' Tom said. He stretched and sighed and then he kissed the back of my neck. By the time Simon got to me I was alone on the step.

'Hi Emily,' he said, 'you been here long?'

'About ten minutes.'

'Really? I didn't see you come in.'

He smiled at me.

'God, Rachel and I are pretty stuck over there.' He gestured his head towards the old lady. 'She used to be an actress. Apparently she's got a few stories – just needed an audience.' He wiped his brow as though it had been a narrow escape. 'Yeah, Rachel's got infinite patience,' he said. 'I'm terrible at all this.'

I looked at his thick hair, the elegant cream shirt he wore so casually.

'I don't believe you,' I said. He smiled.

'OK, but I don't really enjoy it. Anyone can put it on. My side of the family's pretty different to this. We're the poor, sane relations.'

But not everyone could do what he did. His easy laugh and the gentle good humour in his eyes seemed to have made him everyone's favourite. People waved over at him and he called back happily, remembering all their names –

'Hey Julian – what've you done with Sal?' The man smiled and pointed out his little girl on the lawn. And then I suppose I wanted his attention back – I expect that was how he made everyone feel. I said the first thing I could think of.

'You say your side of the family's different, but you and Andrea are pretty close, aren't you?'

'Yeah. We are. Andrea's an amazing woman.'

We both heard her laughter drift in from somewhere and we smiled at each other.

'Rache and I owe her a lot for letting us stay here at the moment,' he said. 'I'm lucky I can help out with the new house – repay her a bit.'

Again, I felt ashamed in front of him. His acceptance of Andrea seemed so far beyond me and my love of implications, my critical analysis of that bitter music in her laugh.

He looked away and emptied his glass.

'Look, I thought I might get drunk, Emily, but you're hardly touching yours and it's putting me off.'

I looked down at my full glass and then I tipped my head back and finished it.

'I see,' he said, 'you're fond of the Château Margot. Should I be encouraging you?'

'Oh, I'll do it anyway,' I told him. I laughed.

'Always laughing,' he said. Funny the different impressions people get.

That was when Rachel stretched her long, brown arm between us –

'Hi, I'm Rachel,' she said.

She had a smooth American accent. No one had mentioned she was American. I felt very pale beside her, conscious I stay out too late at night. She had freckles and pink lips, she looked like something the sun burnt, something the wind blew over, while I am just an idea for a girl. She was tall and narrow and sweet smelling and she made you think of a glass of cool water. I licked the wine off my lips.

'Emily,' I said.

'Hey, careful – you'll stain your dress.' She pointed where a large, dark drop of wine was running down the side of my glass. I put it down. 'Such a pretty dress,' she said. 'I think I have one like it.'

She looked away for a moment and seemed to be smiling fondly, dreamily at the laughter of the old actress. Loose wisps of hair curled lovingly around her neck. She sighed and turned back to us.

'Simon, would you mind getting me some painkillers?'

Simon flinched as though she had hit him.

'Have you got a headache, darling?'

'Just a little one,' she said. She rubbed her temples. 'This is only a little one.'

Something passed between them and changed the tone of Simon's voice.

'Right. Back in a moment,' he said, sounding older, quieter.

When he had gone inside, Rachel sat down on the step beside me.

'So, Emily, how are things with you and Tom?' she asked. 'He's gorgeous, I think. First time I saw him I thought "*you're* going to break a few hearts before you're thirty." Know what I mean?'

I smiled.

'So, are you serious about him?' She laughed, '*God,* Emily – you don't have to answer that. I should mind my own business, right? I'm in*cur*able. I'm always getting myself in trouble that way. I have to know *everything*. Simon says it's because of my job – I'm a costume designer – because of spending all day sewing on tiny pearls or sequins, looking for little pins.' She mimed, scrabbling desperately around on the floor in front of her, her eyes narrowed. There was something slightly hysterical about her and I was not sure I liked her. Then she looked up, smiling her neat smile. 'He says I've developed an unnatural eye for detail. Maybe he's right. Yeah, little things are always visible to me.'

She looked away again. The music seemed to swell in on us and I wondered if it had just been turned on again or if it had been playing all the time without my noticing it. She moved her foot in time for a moment. I watched the tendons in the slim, brown ankle.

'I like your ring,' I told her.

She tilted her hand and the diamond flashed for us.

'You do? Simon found it in Paris for me. He looked all over for just the right thing. After all – I'll be wearing it the rest of my life.' Her laugh trickled into its great pool of certainty.

'Exactly,' I said. 'It has to be right.'

'And it is. Listen Emily, I'm sorry to flake out on you, but my head . . .' She rubbed her temples again. 'I'm going to take a rest for a while – get out of this heat.'

She got up and her flowery perfume poured over me with some of the heat of her body. It felt intimate breathing it in. I said I hoped she would feel better soon and I listened to her footsteps retreating into the shade of the house. I was glad she had gone. At some point her shoes stopped and I heard her talking to Simon, though I could not make out the words. There was the sound of a kiss.

I smiled – as if the fact of their love was an old friend I could not shake off. I knew there was no place for my disappointment and I brushed it away with the grass on my skirt. Rachel is lucky, I thought, and I hope they are happy.

Then I got up and walked away across the garden towards Tom and Jay, who had just arrived.

'We haven't seen you for ages, Jamie,' Andrea was saying. 'What've you been up to?'

Jay smiled shyly.

'Oh, you know, Mrs Raine.' The sun was shining on his blond stubble. His eyes were red and deep-set – drug user's eyes which look like they have seen too many emergencies and are trying to get somewhere less exposed. I felt embarrassed for him, embarrassed by his urgent grin in all that reclining laughter,

'*Do* I know?' Andrea giggled. 'Yes, I probably do.' She had no idea. She squeezed his arm indulgently and walked away to her guests.

A generation gap can make you feel so isolated. Being eighteen, nineteen, twenty is a strange territory between adults and children. Before it you dream about getting there, afterwards you reminisce. But it's all illusion, it's that deserted tropical island in the magazine you think you'd like to run away to – beautiful, luscious, ruleless – but lonely.

I saw my mother standing by a man with a thick, grey beard. He was talking hard at her and she was nodding. I waved at her and she smiled back nervously. She has never been comfortable socially – she prefers to be inside doing the food, the washing-up. I expected she would go soon.

'Brought you a present,' Jay said. He resumed his usual round-shouldered slouch which meant he could look up at Tom even though he was taller.

'Yeah?' Tom said. Jay rooted around in both pockets of his shirt and took out a neatly rolled joint. Tom smiled at him and then looked at me. He looked thinner, younger in broad daylight. I had hardly ever seen him in daylight – our relationship took place at night, when the bars were open. His own eyes were sad and tired looking, thinly glazed with this new excitement.

'You coming?' he said.

'Sure,' I told him. We walked out on to the street to smoke the joint.

We ate lunch on rugs which Simon and Andrea had laid out on the grass. There were salads and bread and meat and cheeses on the long table and everyone took what they wanted and chose a rug to sit on. Rachel did not come out to eat. She didn't appear for the rest of the day. At one point I saw Simon carry a plate in to her. She had not come to supper at our house because of a migraine and I remembered Simon mentioning she had been in hospital before they got married. I wondered if there was something serious wrong with her. When he came out he was smiling a little too brightly, holding a football. Two odd looking teams formed of old, young and middle-aged men and women and a game started at the far end of the garden. Some people lay back on the rugs and sunbathed or fell asleep or just drank wine and smoked and talked more. Soft shouts came over from the game. Gradually people left and the afternoon light got thicker and yellower and the wind stopped altogether.

Andrea came over to the rug where I was sitting. She had just taken my mother out to the car.

'So,' she said, sitting herself down beside me, 'd'you think she enjoyed herself? I don't think she did – she's always thought I was rather frivolous, your mother. *Still*, it's been a beautiful afternoon – weatherwise.' She leant back on her elbows and pulled her skirt up just over her knees so her legs were in the sun. Her skin was deep brown, wrinkled around the knees and I thought of all the distant places she had lived in, the heat she had soaked up. I would have liked her from the start if it hadn't been for her bitterness.

She ran her eyes over the garden and the house.

'Funny leaving this place,' she said. 'It's so many endings in one – divorce.'

'Are you sad to go?'

'Yes and no, Emily. Yes and no. In a sense this was our only family house – Tom and his sister had a couple of happy, stable years here at least. It's the only one that wasn't always a work in progress.'

Tom had never mentioned he had a sister. I looked down at my white arms and a bird shadow slid across my lap.

'Julia's happy, though – I think, "living with Daddy". God knows. They've always been thick as thieves, those two. I leave them to it. I get the odd phone call. Odd phone calls. You settle for things as you get older, Emily.'

I suppose I did like her just then – I liked her mixture of humour and sadness. She sighed.

'Look at my Simon.' We turned and watched him for a moment – unaware of himself, laughing, pushing his sleeves, his hair out of the way, like a child. 'He really keeps me alive. He's great, isn't he? So gentle. He really puts other people before himself.'

I couldn't have known, then, how right she was.

'He's lovely,' I said. I didn't want to look at him any more.

'Jesus – I wonder what your mother thinks. She knows Tony. What did she tell you about him? Just out of interest.'

'She said he didn't believe in God,' I told her.

Andrea tipped her head back and laughed hard.

'*Wonderful,*' she said. She refilled her glass from the bottle beside her and offered me some more. I noticed her hand was unsteady.

'Doesn't believe in God . . . he fucked *everything,* Emily – except me, of course. But then he always was contrary. I should've known it the moment I met him. It was at an English literature lecture – "The Romantic Poets" – and there was this rather gorgeous young man in the row in front of me. Wavy brown hair. He read a book the whole way through – *Big Bang Theory.* She laughed again and pushed all her hair back. 'Ironic, really – that title.

'Anyway, I'm sure you've heard enough of this witchery.'

I didn't say anything, because I really didn't want to hear it. I thought about my mother's calm face when she and Ellie argue –

'You're tired, Ellie. Why don't you go to bed?'

'I'm not tired. I'm not *tired,* for Christ's sake.'

'You'll feel better after a good night's rest.'

I suppose we are all a bit frightened of other people, in my family. The spark caught and Andrea looked at me angrily.

'Too much for you, Emily? I'm so sorry, but you've got no idea. You don't know what it was like . . . kissing your babies good night with that filthy mouth . . .' She curled her lips as though she had eaten something rotten.

'I know,' I said, 'I'm sorry.'

But why do I have to know? I wanted to say. The truth is, I would like to un-know a few things.

'Andrea, it's been gorgeous,' a voice said from above, 'but I think Susie and I are going to make a move.'

'What? But the party's not over, Ian. Jesus, in the old days you never stopped till your head hit the table.'

He laughed. 'Susie turns the computer off now when that happens.'

She got up and kissed her friends goodbye.

'What's happened to us all, Suze? We got old.'

I looked over at Tom. He was saying goodbye to Jay by the gate. I imagined Andrea had always said too much. I saw her picking up a little Tom – 'Oh, mind Mummy's hair, darling – she's got to look sexy for Daddy or Daddy'll run off and leave us, won't he?'

'Tom?' Andrea called out. 'Can I have a word?'

He said something to Jay and then he put out his cigarette and came over.

'I've got a surprise for you,' Andrea said.

His brow furrowed.

'Dad's just called and he's coming by to take you out for supper.'

'What, tonight? Now?' He looked at me to check – the immediacy was unintelligible to him.

Andrea looked at her watch.

'In about ten minutes, darling.'

Tony came through the gate an hour later. I was helping to clear up and I saw a man standing in the driveway. He walked over to one of the fences and shook it as if he was checking how much strain it would take and then he cleared his throat and walked towards the house. Simon was dismantling the long table.

'Is that Tom's Dad?' I asked. Simon looked over. The man walking towards us really could have been him in twenty years' time. It made me nervous. I thought how strange and powerful the face of her young husband must be to Andrea – to see it live again and laughing in front of her, so soon after Tony had left for good.

'Tony!' Simon shouted. He jogged over to him and they hugged each other. I could hear them laughing and Tony kept slapping Simon's shoulder. I took a tray of glasses into the house and wished I had left an hour ago. Who needs another complicated family? They came into the kitchen after me.

'Tony, this is Emily – Tom's girlfriend,' Simon said. He smiled at me, as if he had interpreted my reserve as shyness. I did not want to meet this Christmas present of a father. He put his hand out.

'Tom's girlfriend?' He smiled knowingly. 'Nice to meet you, Emily – I'm Tom's father.'

It was a perfect smile, his warm, brown face crushing out good humour from the chinks of blue eyes, the flash of white teeth.

'Where's Andrea?'

'I'll get her,' Simon said.

I put some of the glasses in the dishwasher, glad to have an occupation, and listened to Tony lighting a cigarette. I could tell he was smiling, I could feel it on my neck, on the backs of my legs. His smile curled all the way round a room.

'So, are you going to come out for dinner with us, Emily?'

'I – well, I could, but I'm sure Tom would like to see you on his own.'

'Boring old Dad? I couldn't deprive him of you.' I heard Tom in the smooth voice.

'Hiya Tony,' Andrea said.

She had redone her hair. Suddenly I felt worried for her. Tony didn't say anything, he just walked over and hugged her and I admired and hated his subtle sense of occasion. How much living do you have to do, I wondered, to get a sense of occasion like that?

'Tom's just coming – he's having a quick shower,' she told him.

'Great.'

She sighed. 'Oh, come on then, let's all have a drink together. Emily, are any of those glasses clean?'

I handed her four of them and she kissed my cheek, which I took to be an apology for the tenseness of our earlier conversation. Or perhaps she was simply gathering allies in front of her ex-husband. I was beginning to see how her simplest gestures creaked with significance. Nothing was stated openly by her – every feeling that crossed her face naturally, she immediately snatched up and soaked in her own bitterness. She would then restate it to plead her case: wronged, vulnerable, angry –

each expression a frantic caricature of its natural self.

She forced everyone around her into playing the same game. Even Simon seemed to have resorted to a forced show of chivalry in front of her. Grand-scale sympathy for her grand-scale sadness, I suppose. He smiled brilliantly and took the wine glasses from her as if they were too heavy for her to carry. I was surprised to see how much Tony's presence had unsettled Simon. He seemed torn between the two of them. He gave Tony an apologetic smile.

Tony put his hand lightly on my back and we all walked out to the garden again. We stood in the evening sun with our glasses.

'God, it looks beautiful. I miss England,' Tony said. 'When are you leaving the place?'

Andrea smiled into her drink and then looked at him.

'Three weeks today,' she said. 'And you don't miss *England* – you miss June and July – that's not England.'

Tony laughed.

I did feel sorry for Andrea. Why pick this of all days to turn up? I thought. I got the impression Tony would not allow her a clean exit.

'Work going well, Tony?' Simon asked.

He smoothed back his silver hair.

'Sure – not bad. I'm working on a new sitcom, actually.'

'Ah – plenty of material to draw on,' Andrea said.

'You could put it like that. I wouldn't.'

'Well, there'd be no comedy if the characters all agreed with each other.'

'Indeed.'

Andrea mimicked him: '*Indeed*,' she said pompously.

'Bloody ex-wives – can't take them anywhere.' She elbowed me and laughed, then she looked back at Tony. 'Oh, but that's the *point* of ex-wives, isn't it? You don't *have* to take them anywhere – don't even have to contact them for six weeks – and they still go on dutifully being your ex-wife. Till death do you part. Sensible arrangement – realistic ring to it. How is Ilaria, anyway?'

'She's well – thanks for asking, Andrea.'

Andrea laughed. 'Oh, you're so dignified, Tony, aren't you?' she said.

I heard Simon's shoe move on the paving stone. I could feel him searching for something to say.

'Oh look, why don't I piss off and get Tom before there's a bust-up,' Andrea said.

She walked into the house leaving the three of us behind. Simon looked at me anxiously.

'Don't worry, Simon,' Tony said. 'It's a bit soon, that's all. There's a rhythm to everything. Give it a bit of time.

'I do hope we haven't embarrassed you, Emily.' He gave me the smile and I felt myself returning it involuntarily.

'No, of course not,' I said. He really was impeccable.

When Tom came down, Tony told him he was taking the two of us out for dinner. We could pick anywhere in London, he said, anywhere we liked.

The restaurant was on the top floor of a hotel, with a view over the City. In front of us, soft in the distance, was the dome of St Paul's with the City a shadowy cluster of skyscrapers behind it. To the left the river curved round and you could just see the Houses of Parliament lit up orange against the sky.

'Quite a show,' Tony said. 'That really is something.'

We all stared, but to me that whole view was lost to the blur of peripheral focus. Just then my mind picked over and over one tiny memory. The memory was this:

Sitting on the step outside Andrea's kitchen. The sun on my legs, the glass of wine in my hand. Simon's face looking down at me –

'Hi Emily,' he said, 'you been here long?'

'About ten minutes.'

'Really? I didn't see you come in.'

It meant he had looked out for me. Are you so pathetically glad to be noticed by him? I asked myself. Yes, was the answer. I gripped the napkin in my lap –

'Really? I didn't see you come in.' – And then he had smiled at me. But you know you are imagining it all, really, I told myself. And you have no business imagining anything. I wanted very desperately to get outside and walk, not to be stuck at that table.

Tom and his father held the huge white menus and carried on looking out over the river. The menus made them look like little children. It was starting to get darker outside. I felt tired suddenly and I folded my hands in my lap. When I looked up, the waiter had filled our glasses.

'So,' Tony said. He rubbed his hands together expectantly. He seemed to have made ready for something a few times now. 'So, how've you been, Tom?'

'Great.'

'That's fantastic. Julia sends her love.'

I looked at Tom to see what reaction his sister's name provoked. His face registered nothing; it was as blank as his father's. The absence of emotion shows obscenely sometimes, like the gap of daylight where a missing limb should be.

Tony raised the white menu again.

'Shall we order? I'm starving,' he said. He called the waiter over without asking if we were ready. We ordered and gave up the menus. It felt empty without them.

'So, you're both at the same stage, are you? It's so hard to tell with girls – you all look so sophisticated. Gets us into trouble,' Tony said, smiling at me. The smile became satirical. 'You been thinking *long* and *deep* about university, too?'

'I thought I might go to film school actually,' Tom said.

He had obviously never said this to his father before. Tony looked at him.

'Really? It's a tough world, Tom.'

'Yeah, I know.' He looked out of the window at the darkening sky. 'I could write scripts, though – just like you, Dad.'

'You could . . .' Tony said, 'of course you could.'

The air conditioning was on too high in the restaurant and it felt cold. Tom looked intensely at his napkin, waiting for Tony to say something. Tony stretched and yawned.

'God, I'm an old man, Emily,' he said suddenly. 'Today has wiped me out. I can't do this running all over the city thing any more. I had a breakfast meeting with a producer, lunch – if you can call a few prawns lunch – with my agent, and now here I am with you two sprightly things. I need a hot bath and a book. I'm sorry – I'm not much company.'

'It's good to see you, Dad,' Tom said, 'it's been a very long time.'

'You're right, Tom. I know that. You'll see how it is when

you get older – it takes a lot of time and energy to make life run smoothly. Things get . . . *postponed*, when they shouldn't.'

He looked at me again, almost imploringly.

'We've just bought this great place in Barcelona, but, you know, it *"needed-a-lot-of-work"*. God, we've knocked walls through, put in new bathrooms . . .' He blew up at his forehead and flicked his hand in front of his eyes, clearing the rubble away. 'A *lot* of work,' he said.

'Houses, houses, building, building, houses, houses,' Tom said, nodding his head down in time as if he was falling asleep on the table. He lit a cigarette.

'Hey, our food'll be here soon.'

'I'll put it out when it arrives, Dad.'

– and with that they established their pattern. Throughout dinner, dull, brittle exchanges strained around their live differences.

It was completely dark by the time we ordered coffee.

'You don't eat, you girls,' Tony said, looking at me. 'Won't you have some pudding?'

I shook my head. It had been an uncomfortable meal and I had no appetite.

'Trying to stay slim and beautiful?' he asked, nodding, folding away the menu.

'Em's not like that,' Tom said. 'I wouldn't go out with a girl like that.'

'Nothing wrong with looking after yourself,' Tony said. He touched my hand.

'She isn't like that, though – like Ilaria, always at the gym – personal trainers, facials. All that shit.'

'Well, Emily's just naturally beautiful, then. Lucky her.'

He smiled graciously at me and Tom sat back, his face red. 'Lucky *us,*' Tony said.

The waiter brought the coffee. When he had put it down and come back with the sugar, Tony said, 'Come on, Tom – this is supposed to be a good thing. I didn't mean for it to get like this. It was supposed to be – a good thing.

'We should've seen a film or something,' he said. 'I thought this would be fun, that's all. Obviously not.' Again he looked at me. He needed women to forgive him.

Tom was quiet for a moment, and then he put his napkin on the table and said, 'So, how is Ilaria, anyway?' just the way Andrea had.

His father laughed without smiling.

'Actually, I haven't seen her for four or five weeks, Tom – if it makes you feel any better.' He rubbed his hands up and down his face as if he was washing it.

When we got on to the street, Tony hailed a cab.

'Mind if I take this one? I'm exhausted and I expect you two are going on somewhere.' He put his foot inside and then turned around and handed Tom a few £50 notes. 'Let me know about that film school idea,' he said. He slammed the door and sank back in the seat. We watched his shiny hair catch each street light as the taxi crossed the river.

Chapter four

I always thought there was nothing safer than lying in the arms of someone you don't love. When Tom looked at me and his eyes softened I helped myself to all the pleasure of being loved with none of the cost to myself. It wasn't new to me. When I think about the boys I have slept with I know it's been the same every time – I've never wanted anyone and it has made me interesting. I have no illusions about why they want me. It might sound like I'm self-sufficient – I'm not, I just have a talent for loneliness. There is nothing calculating about it, it's natural, like knowing how to draw.

My friend Nina and I discovered loneliness. She was my best friend when I was six. Her father had moved to America with his girlfriend and started a new family. There were brothers and sisters she had never met. Nina was the Daddy and I was the Mummy. We lay in bed together with no clothes on and Nina used to move up and down on top of me, going 'Ugh, Ugh' the way she had seen it done in a film.

I remember when we first did it. Dad looked angry when Nina arrived that day, because it was Mum's day for teaching First Communion and I knew he would have liked to take me to see Tomasz. Irena had been crying when we left last time.

'It's fine – it's just you didn't *mention* it. I just wish you let me *know* these things,' I heard him say to Mum.

'I'd have thought it would be easier for you, darling. Take them off to the Disney thing in South Ken – I booked some tickets. I shouldn't worry – they go off for hours together.'

He came in while we were still playing our game. He leant his head round the door and said:

'How'd you like to go to the cinema, you two? Feeling too lazy?' He yawned and looked out of the window. We lay very still under the covers. Nina was heavy on top of me. I could feel her heart going through the bones in her chest and our tummies felt sticky together.

'Yes, please,' I said.

'Right, well get ready, then. I'll see you downstairs.' He let the door swing shut and Nina and I got dressed quickly without saying anything to each other.

The week before, our au pair had brought boys back a few times and one night Mum had an argument with her and told her to get out. I did not know exactly what she had done, but I knew it was very, very wrong. Perhaps she would have to go to prison. I had never seen Mum angry like that before. She cried for a long time afterwards. The au pair left some of her things behind – some make-up and a pair of high-heeled boots. They were powerful things. I touched some of them a few days afterwards. When we left for the film, I put the high-heeled boots on. I didn't know why, but I did. It made Nina giggle – this was what she liked about me. Dad didn't notice. They were dark red boots and the heels were thin like spikes. I had big feet and they almost fitted.

In the cinema, people looked at the boots and then stared at Dad. He didn't notice that either. When we got to our seats he said he was just going out to make a phone call. I knew he was calling her. The film was a cartoon and I watched the pink elephants and the cute lions and I felt like a counterfeit child. My shoulder was always waiting for the big hand to land on it and throw me out.

Dad was waiting outside the door at the end. He looked worn out.

'Right, go to the loo then, both of you, before we head back,' he said – as if he was properly in charge. I remember how in the toilets there was a poster by the hand-drying machine. It was a picture of a little Indian girl, very thin and dusty and tired, who looked to me like she had dressed up in her mother's clothes: 'Stop the trade!' the poster said, and then stuff underneath which I couldn't understand. I stared at the little girl's face for a while and then the fake rose smell of the soap in there started making me sick.

I remember that poster. I am not susceptible to much, but that poster still gets me – when I think about myself standing there, looking up at it. I think it is the mixture of knowing and not knowing which the image contains – a child held between the polarities of innocence and disgust, with no vocabulary to express her confusion. I think about the high-heeled boots – part show for my friend and part protest to Dad. Now I think I wanted him to know just how much innocence I had lost, just how unlike the other children at the cinema I was. But he didn't notice, he bought us an ice-cream for staying in our seats while he made his phone call.

The rose air freshener, the sickly chocolate ice-cream. I think that day awoke the first half-conscious sense that what Dad was doing with Irena, what he had included me in, would never ever wash off.

Nina and I both looked older than we were. We both took coke together the first time, when we were fourteen. Nina's older brother gave it to her for her birthday. I slept with him and she slept with his friend. It was the first time for both of us. Afterwards she said, 'We're really married, now', and we laughed and laughed about it. It was the loneliest thing I had ever heard and I didn't see her for a while after that.

I felt lonely with Tom, but I had begun to like him. I felt sorry for him – for having a father like Tony who had made everything seem so cheap and a mother like Andrea who had made everything seem so precious. His cheap grin, her bankrupt's laugh. Tom had no idea of the value of anything – any kind gesture or false loyalty. He blew the fifties his father had given him on a pair of trainers and some Es. We went out the next few nights after that dinner with Tony and it felt like he kept his arm around me most of the time.

'God, Emily, this is like a *serious* relationship, isn't it?' my friend Sarah said. 'Tom is a changed man – he looks smitten.

He won't even flirt with *me* any more.' We were sitting by the bar at Raf's. I looked over at Tom talking with his friends and I wished he had never met me.

He drove me home those nights and we had sex in the car. I watched his face on the seat, the eyes closed, the beautiful jaw gritted so that a muscle twitched in his cheek, and while I moved I thought I don't love you, I don't love you, I don't love you – like a paraplegic trying to feel the pinprick on the sole of his foot.

The next night I told him I wasn't feeling well. I stayed on my own instead. I wasn't enjoying Raf's any more and sitting in Tom's car was just waiting in traffic. I didn't want to see my own friends either. I read during the day and at night I took the tube out to the Embankment and walked by the river and then through the city, until I was tired. London glints at night – like jewellery and like hidden knives. It was exciting to walk through it alone seeing things both ways at once.

It felt good getting into bed so tired that my eyes closed over me. I slept late into the afternoon and came down when the sun had already warmed the stone on the kitchen floor. For three days, I managed not to see anyone at all.

I heard my parents talking that night.

'Just stop fussing, Jane,' my father said.

'I'm not. I'm really not. I mean is it drugs? She's not eating, you know. I leave things – yoghurts, chicken – they're never touched.'

'Probably *lurve*,' Dad said. 'Some local spotty Hamlet.' I could hear him straightening out his newspaper the way he does when he wants to send my mother away.

'It's hard, John if you don't have anything to believe in. I couldn't do it.'

'It always comes back to God, doesn't it?'

There was a pause.

'Well – yes,' my mother said.

'Oh, don't do that, Jane – not that voice. I can only tolerate it all because *thankfully* you don't often use that *bloody* voice. Anyway, I wouldn't worry about her immortal soul – I'm sure you've earned enough air miles for all of us.' I listened to her tidying up for a while.

Ellie and I used to go to church with Mum. I thought about how we hadn't been for a long time. Ellie was too little to understand, but I had liked it. I liked it for all the reasons I would hate it now – for the soft way the priests looked at you, the way they rested their hand on your head, meaning all was forgiven. I even did my first Communion in a lovely white dress, but by the time it got round to Ellie, we had stopped going. It's just Mum now. She does the flowers and she does the First Communion classes for other people's children. Dad won't go. I don't know why Ellie and I stopped, though. I expect they had an argument about it. It's one of the things we have never talked about – like their bedroom and how Dad keeps his clothes in the wardrobe, but always sleeps in the spare room.

(The spare room is where all the books go that won't fit on the shelves in the hall any more. I suppose I don't like to think of my father in there, white haired, exiled, cuddled up to piles of old history books, dusty biographies.)

A while ago I found a little crucifix in my sister's room. I was looking for something she had borrowed and there it was on her dressing table, beside the sparkly mascara and the fake tan. I wondered where she had got it. I wanted a crucifix once. I thought I would say prayers secretly in my room in front of it. Maybe I had seen a film about a nun. Maybe I was the same sort of age as Ellie. I remember going to the jewellers on the high street and looking into all the glass cases, at the watches and the engagement rings. I could see my stupid face in the glass, pretending to know what it was doing. Then the girl came and asked if she could help me. I told her what I was looking for and I brought my thumb and forefinger together to show her it was an insignificant thing I wanted. She unlocked a drawer with one of the little keys that hung off her belt. There were four or five crosses pinned on the velvet.

'There you are,' she told me. 'I'm afraid we haven't got any with the little man on it.'

I like memories like that – I like it when my seriousness gets slapped in the face. I have an idea that it's good for your character.

In my family, God makes people say strange things – I learnt that early on. People make loud jokes while everything in the room gets quieter. Even the chairs get quieter. Like at my first Communion, when my Uncle Peter, who had wanted to be a monk after university, said, 'Ah! Jesus will be very *pleased* with us, Emily,' whenever he took a slice of cake. Uncle Peter is enormously fat. They wouldn't have him at the monastery for some reason.

I turned Ellie's crucifix around in my fingers, looking at the tiny arms and hands. Then I saw whatever she had borrowed and I picked it up and went out of the room. I was glad to shut the door.

Things get spoilt so easily. I have sometimes wondered why, when I was Ellie's age, I wanted to say my prayers in secret. Dad wouldn't actually have stopped me going to church. He would just have rolled his eyes. But it would have been enough. I have always been secretive, because when people know what you care about it all gets spoilt. You start to see it through their eyes and whatever it is – a doll, a person, even a God – it looks ridiculous. There you are suddenly, behind glass, observed by scientists. A human animal, whose behaviour is not so beautifully remote as it thought, from the need for food, the fear of attack in the night.

We all know how to spoil things for other people. But still we carry on speculating, guessing at the limits of other people's love. We all feel each other looking. Maybe it was fear of my own capacity to judge and ridicule that shoved me out of Ellie's room away from her little crucifix. After all, what's the point of documenting the limits of love, its pitiful motivations – are there so many better things to do in life than love blindly?

The day I saw Simon I was up earlier than usual. The house looked clean and smelt of furniture polish. I lay down in the sitting room reading a book and hearing the cars go by the double glazing with their sound a bit like the sea. When I looked up, Simon was walking past the window. He was looking straight ahead. He took his hands out of his pockets and then put them in again. He gave a quick look at our front door. I went up to the landing to see him better. Rachel was coming quickly down the street after him, holding the car keys. Her smooth, sculpted face was smiling, her hair was tied back behind her ears. She called something out and Simon smiled and took the keys from her when she reached him. They went through the gate of the new house together.

It was a clear day and it looked a bit cooler than it had been all week. On the news they had said it was the longest heat wave in twenty years. It was impossible to believe that weather would end.

About ten minutes later, I walked past Andrea's place thinking I would go and get a paper for Dad. He was lecturing that day and he would be glad to do the crossword with his drink in the evening. I do these things for Dad. On this level it is possible to feel and show love for him – by acknowledging his habits, pouring his drink, being thanked. It's better than nothing. The sound of hammering came from the house and I heard one of the builders shouting, 'Ready!' Drills started up. I did not see Rachel or Simon and I went on to the newsagent's.

When I came out with the paper, I saw them going into the hardware shop across the road. I could make them out behind the shop window. They were looking at the shelves of paint and checking the list in Rachel's hand. Rachel did all the talking to the shop assistant and Simon looked up and down at the cans of paint and then came over to the doorway to look out. I moved in behind the bus shelter which had a smeared, little window. There was graffiti all over the glass and Simon slid in and out of the letters. I was afraid and fascinated to see him lost in his own thoughts – in the egotism of my imagination, I only ever pictured him talking to Rachel to excite my jealousy, or talking to me.

After a while Rachel called him back and they made some kind of arrangement with the store assistant, looking at their watches and deciding on a time. When it was agreed, they came out and walked towards the café over the road. They sat down at a table outside. A blue car obscured them for a moment and then passed. She looked at him softly and then he stroked the hair off her face and kissed her mouth. It looked like a habit of theirs.

When I looked down, I saw I had crushed up the paper in my hand. The crossword was torn and I knew Dad would want a new one now. I smiled at myself and tried to smooth it out. I watched the waiter bring them some coffee and I thought how happy they looked drawing something on a napkin, deciding things about Andrea's house. They made big gestures in the air, knocking walls through, making archways. They were like the Lebanese couple, with their plans on the ground in front of them.

This felt different, though – I could not put myself in this dream. I knew it was a mistake to look. Following people, for God's sake, I thought. I had tears in my eyes and I wanted to go home. I wanted to be back on the sofa in the sitting room with the cars going quietly past. After a while, I straightened out the paper a bit more and walked out. I held my back very straight and went down the road. I was crying and it was hard to stop my shoulders shaking where they could still have seen me. When I crossed the road, a car stopped suddenly and let me go in front of it. The woman smiled at me.

Our road felt very quiet. The light in the trees looked unnatural, as if the sun had come out in the middle of the night. I could hear my blood going and my legs felt tired a very long way below me. My mouth was dry. I sat down for a moment on the wall beside me.

'Hey Emily? What's the matter?' It was Simon's voice shouting after me. I smiled at him, watching him come down the road. There was no point in trying to get the tears off my face.

'I'm OK,' I said when he got to me. I was smiling hard.

Simon looked back up the road.

'I'm – we're having a coffee at that place on the corner. Forgot my wallet.' He held up his empty hands.

I imagined with a sense of dread how Rachel had seen me from their table and said:

'Hey isn't that Emily – Tom's girlfriend?'

'Is it? Oh yeah.'

'She looks upset. Simon, I think she's got a crush on you, you know. Just go and make sure she's all right, darling – I'll order the coffee.'

'Oh, I can't. I'll embarrass her.'

'Tell her you're running for your wallet, or something – just passing. Go on. Poor thing.'

Simon lowered his hands to his sides and smiled at me.

'I'm an idiot,' he said, '*always* forgetting things.'

'Me too,' I told him. I hardly knew what we were talking about. I tried to stand up, but I had to sit back against the wall again. I laughed at myself.

'Emily, what's happened?' Simon said. 'Is it Tom?'

For a moment, I couldn't think what he meant.

'Tom?' I said. Then it made me laugh. I laughed in two ways: first at myself and then at what it made me think about human nature.

'I just thought – I don't know, I just thought it might be an argument or something. Love does terrible things to your nervous system, doesn't it?'

'Listen, I'm fine.'

My head had started to feel better and I tried standing up again.

'Look at that,' I said. 'Complete recovery.'

'Maybe you just need something to eat or something.'

'Exactly.'

I felt his mind drift away again, back to Rachel, back to marriage, to habitual intimacy. He was kissing her mouth now – right there in front of me. The pain felt too large for my arms and legs. In a few minutes I would be at home, I told myself. I looked back at him, taking him in from his shoes up. My eyes stopped at his shirt pocket.

'There's your wallet,' I said. He looked down and laughed – nervously at first and then sadly. He sat down on the wall.

'It was just – I saw you and you looked so . . . I just wanted to make sure you were OK. *OK*?'

'OK,' I said. We laughed and I wiped my hand across my eyes.

'Well, are you?'

'No.'

We laughed again.

'Well, thank God I was around.' He waved his hand. 'Any time.'

What does it matter, I thought – you've made a fool of yourself and that's that. For a second I let myself imagine it had been me at that café table – *my* husband, his hand stroking my face, the ring against my cheek. The crazy thoughts made my face feel red and I was afraid he knew exactly what I was thinking.

'Look, I'll see you soon, Simon,' I told him. 'I really should get back.'

He stood up.

'Tom coming round, is he?'

'I don't think so, no. I should really go, though.'

Why did he have to keep mentioning Tom? I knew he thought we were stupid children. He brushed his hands off hard on his jeans.

'See you, then. Hope you feel better.'

'Thanks. Good luck with all the work on the house,' I said. I smiled and went back home.

When I got in, I could hear Ellie laughing. The TV was on in the kitchen and cigarette smoke was curling up the stairs. More books had been delivered for Dad. They were in a pile by his study door. I put the paper down on top of them for him and thought: what a life. I wondered if he was happy with all his words.

I walked down to the kitchen, wondering who was there. Ellie and Tom were playing cards on the kitchen table and Jay was rolling a joint. He had his foot up on an empty chair and he took it off when he saw me.

'All right?' Tom said. He didn't look up from his cards. He was smiling.

'I'm telling you, I've never seen a hand like this.'

'Bluffing,' Ellie said. She had sounded very confident and it made her giggle.

'Hi, Jay,' I said. I kissed him on the cheek.

'All right, gorgeous?'

Then Tom gave me his cheek, keeping his eyes on the cards. 'Vital moment,' he said. He made a kissing sound near my face.

I made myself a cup of tea and sat down at the table with them. The card game had finished.

'Your little sister's a shark,' Tom said. 'There's a vicious streak somewhere in your family.'

'There is not,' Ellie said. 'I'm just cleverer than you. People aren't being vicious just because you lose – don't you know that?'

'Why aren't you at school anyway?' Tom said.

'It's the holidays, durr.'

He laughed.

Ellie was wearing my lipstick and a pair of my jeans. Her hair had green streaks in it.

'What's going on with your hair?' I asked her.

'Becks did it for me. Cool, isn't it?' She swung it around as she got up and it made me smile and think how much I loved her. 'I might do it all green if I feel like it.'

'You'll look like a frog,' Tom told her.

'I will not.' She looked embarrassed and I saw her glance in the mirror over the cupboard.

Jay sighed.

'You people are *way* too hectic.' He lit the joint and took a few drags and then held it out to Tom. Ellie took it, stretching her arm in front of his. I didn't say anything. What is there that I could say? Jay had been rolling up on one of Mum's books. It was called *The Habit of Prayer*.

After a while, we lay out on the grass in our garden. Ellie was laughing a lot at everything Tom said. It seemed to encourage him and his voice went on in the background more than I had heard it for weeks. I lay back and thought maybe I could hear the banging from the house across the road. The air was so still our cigarette smoke hung in clouds over us and then drifted towards the bushes and was lost.

Later on, Ellie took Tom inside to find something to drink. I stretched out further on the grass.

'So, where've you been, Em?' Jay said.

'Me? Nowhere really – just haven't felt like going out.'

'Yeah? Everything cool?' He sounded like a friendly enemy.

'I'm fine, Jay,' I said. I wanted to ask him what was so great about going out anyway – didn't it ever wear off, this thrill of knowing the right people, getting in ahead of the queue. I thought about Simon stroking the hair off Rachel's face.

'I just think Tom's like *worried* about you and shit. I know it's like not my place and everything . . . Hey, don't look like that,' he said, 'he cares about you. You're a weird girl, Em. D'you know that? D'you know how many girls would die to be with Tom? Any girl I get near, they're like: "Who's your friend".'

'Yes,' I told him, 'I know all that.'

Ellie and Tom came out of the house.

'Lunch?' Tom looked at me. 'You coming out?'

'Can I come?' Ellie said. Tom was still looking at me. He had a way of knocking you out with his expectations. He made you see stars with those eyes of his, that hand picking at the hem of his shirt.

'Look, I'm not really that hungry. I might meet up with you later on.' I just wanted to lie there very still and quiet – as if any sudden movement might shatter the picture I was keeping of Simon smiling gently at me a little while ago.

'I'll get my bag,' Ellie told him.

'Ellie, I think Mum might not want you to go.'

'Lucky she's not here, then, isn't it?' She ran into the house to get her bag.

'She's a handful,' Jay said.

'She's fourteen,' I told him. 'D'you understand what I'm saying?'

'Oh chill out, Emily. What has *happened* to you?' Tom said. 'You need to have some fun.' He walked back into the house.

When they had gone, I lay back on the grass. I lay there until it was cooler and the shade from the fence stretched far beyond my feet. There was a smell of cut grass – someone was mowing their lawn a few gardens along. The people next door were sitting outside – you could hear the ice clinking in their glasses. I went upstairs and ran a cool bath and stayed in it for a long time, listening to that lawn mower go up and down.

I heard Ellie come in after a while. She went straight to her room and put her music on. I sank down into the water as I heard her door shut. Tom's mobile had been switched off when I tried it.

Later that night, Ellie was in the kitchen when I came down for a drink. She was putting nail varnish on.

'Have a nice time?' I asked her.

'Mmm?'

'You and Tom and Jay?

She looked up, smiling.

'D'you think Tom could be a model? I do. He's so funny, too.'

'Where did you go?'

'Just to this restaurant. I met Kate and Jamie and Ronnie. Kate looks like a film star, don't you think?'

'She's very beautiful,' I said.

'I think she's the most beautiful girl I've ever seen – except you, I suppose.'

I laughed and poured myself some orange juice.

'I'm nothing special,' I said.

'That's not what Tom says.'

'What else did you do, then?'

'Just chilled out, really. Tom dropped me all the way back afterwards.'

'That was nice of him.'

'Mmm.' She started blowing on her nails to dry the varnish. 'We get on really well – except when he kept saying "This is Emily's little sister" to everyone. It's not like I don't have a name.'

'Don't you think they're all a bit too old for you to be friends with?'

'My friends are always older – Saskia's two years above, you know?'

I let the subject drop and put my trainers on and walked out on to the street.

Sometimes I wonder how well I know myself. How much control I have over what I'm about to do. I walked over the road towards Andrea's place. There were lights on and someone tugged a window closed, but I couldn't see who. Anyone could have been in there.

The front door was propped open with a paint-spattered phone directory and I stepped over it and walked in. There was the good, new smell of wet paint and plaster. It was cool and damp. There was a bare light bulb hanging in the hallway. I could hear someone walking on the floorboards above. I tried to guess from the sound of the shoes if it was a man or a woman. Then I heard Tom's voice shout from the room across the hallway:

'Simon, can we please go? What're you *doing* up there?' I heard the sound of magazine pages being flipped over impatiently and then Tom standing up. I walked softly into the room beside me and stood against the wall, behind the door. Tom's shoes walked out into the hallway. I could hear him tapping his front teeth together the way he did when he was bored. I looked down at my arms and I thought I looked like a ghost in the street light coming through the window. Simon ran down the stairs.

'Just making sure I've shut all the windows,' he said. His voice was slightly breathless, energetic. My eyes locked on the window opposite me and saw it was open.

'Cool. It's not like there's anything to nick, Simon. So, can we go now?' Tom said.

'Two seconds. Just check in here.'

He came into the room towards the window. A few steps from it, something caught his eye – something white and out of place – and he turned and saw me. He was just out of sight of the doorway and for what can only have been a second, he stood still and looked and then he smiled at me – softly.

'OK, let's go,' he called to Tom. They went out and locked the door after them. I listened to them walk away down the pavement. Tom was humming that song he liked.

My face felt hot and I dug my nails into the palms of my hands, waiting for the sound of the car driving away. He had left the window open for me to climb out. He would be polite, it would all be forgotten. I would laugh about it one day when I was old and hideous. It would get packed away neatly with other broken things.

I thought about that au pair – Sylvie her name was – throwing all her things into her big sports bag. She grabbed handfuls of tapes and clattered them all in; shoes – one was wedged under the bed; a pile of dirty clothes. I watched from the landing, feeling the power of it.

'Get *out*!' my mother shouted.

The girl had tears going down her face, her make-up ran in crooked lines like dirty raindrops. She pushed past, smacking her bag on the banisters.

'Strange,' she said as she went down the stairs. It was like a curse. I remember her eyes screwed up at my mother. *'Strange people!'* And when the taxi roared her away and everything was still and my mother was crying quietly, I remember the feeling of peace – of chaos taken away from us.

Then I heard footsteps running up the drive and the door was unlocked. I knew it was Simon. He came in and stood in front of me with his hand resting on the door handle – half in, half out. I looked up at him. I could hear him breathing. I looked around the empty room, the bare light bulb throwing a pool of light in from the hall and the street light streaming towards it with a gap of darkness between.

Then Simon kissed my mouth and I was so tired that this

time my eyes closed over both of us and I heard him say 'Meet me here tomorrow night' in a cracked voice, before he left. I waited and listened to Tom's car drive him away towards the main road.

Chapter five

The next day was a Saturday and our house was full of footsteps and brisk voices. There were sounds of cleaning, lunch, a girl selling oven gloves on the doorstep. Ellie had a friend to stay and they locked themselves up in her room, laughing occasionally over the music. It was too hot to stay in the house. The sun burnt on the carpets. I read in the garden, under the tree and slept most of the afternoon. That heat had been meant for somewhere far away from England – it made you feel lost.

After supper my mother stood up to clear away the plates. She looked slouched and tired. Dad used to try to make her stand up straight – he would put his hand on the small of her back and say 'Ja-ane' , stretching the word out, nipping it up at the end, as if he was her dad who knew better. He has given up now. Her stepfather hit her when she was little, and I think she is still cowering for the next blow. I see her sometimes, alone in the garden, slouched, looking out at her flowers.

I don't always think she's unhappy, though. Sometimes, when she comes back from church it's as if her face is in a softer focus. At those times she has the gentlest smile I have ever seen. Her gentleness is the best thing about her, even though it has been her undoing with Dad. I like to think of her cupping a moth in her hands to let it outside, telling us about heaven when our rabbit died, peeling an apple in one long curl.

Ellie went up to her room to watch TV.

'Good night, darling,' my mother said. My father stretched, looking out of the window.

'Have you put that white in the fridge *already*, Jane? I feel like another glass.'

Dad used to drink too much and you can tell Mum still worries about it. Her voice came out sounding too vague for her.

'Didn't we finish it? I thought we finished it.'

She is like a child sometimes. Dad snorted and walked over to the fridge.

'A *whole* bottle at one sitting? Highly unlikely – high moral tone of a place like this.'

He talks that way when he's going to drink – hard, broken sentences like bits of smashed glass. He took the bottle out. It was misted cold, half full.

'Quite a nice wine,' he said. My mother knocked a fork clattering into the sink. 'A nice, honest, reasonable wine,' he sighed. He rolled his eyes at me as he sat back down at the table. I was his ally tonight for some reason. I knew there was no reason, really.

'Like some, Em?'

'OK,' I said. 'Thanks.'

He poured me a glass.

'What shall we drink to? Got any exams that need toasting?'

'Nope. All done,' I told him.

'My book then,' he said. 'You can never drink too many toasts to a new book.'

'Are you sure about that?'

Dad had his mischievous face on.

'Now hang on. What are you implying? You name one writer – just try – name *one* writer who was also an alcoholic,' he said.

My mother went quietly up the stairs.

'Tell you what, Em – if you can name one,' he raised his voice after her, 'I'll open another bottle.' He laughed at his joke and reached for a bottle of red wine from the rack. He opened it, peeling the foil off on to the remains of the pudding Mum had made. 'Let it breathe,' he said. 'Poor bastard.'

I lit a cigarette and he had one of the small cigars he likes. After a while I looked over at him.

'Is this a special occasion or something?'

He puffed a cloud of smoke into the air.

'Finished my first draft.'

'Dad – that's fantastic. You should've said something.' He mimicked confusion – he just had, after all. 'To Mum, I mean.'

'Ah.' He pulled on the cigar and the end crackled as it burnt. He picked up the bottle of red wine and squinted at the label.

'This is the one thing that useless uncle of yours is any good at, you know – wine.'

'Where is Peter? We haven't seen him for a while.'

Throughout my childhood Uncle Peter had put on shows – great shows of love and imagination for me and Ellie. He left us giggling, in love, full of ice-cream and in-jokes. And then he would disappear. I miss him. Dad snorted.

'Probably having one of his declines.'

'I think he's lonely. Why doesn't he ever have a girlfriend?'

Dad looked at me as though he was frightened – but I knew it was pretend. He has a whole range of pantomime expressions, which set off his apathy to best effect.

'You're not serious,' he said.

'What?'

He laughed a hard, dry laugh, tipping his head back.

'Your Uncle Peter is a *raving* queer, Em. Don't tell me you didn't know that.'

'I didn't know that,' I said.

Dad stood up and tucked the paper under his arm. He was still doing the dry laugh – more quietly now. He held the bottle of red wine in the crook of his elbow, against his chest.

'You're more innocent than I realise, sometimes,' he said. 'How did you get so innocent, Emily?'

He patted my hair before he started up the stairs. I heard him make a sighing noise, as if he was tired from too much laughing, before he reached the hall.

At about ten, I brushed my hair and looked out of my bedroom window towards Andrea's place. The lights were on in two of the upper rooms. A rusty looking cement mixer threw a shadow in the front garden. Simon's car was parked a little way off down the road. It was the time of night when privacy comes down quietly.

I put on my shoes and went softly down the stairs. I was about to do something indelible. There is a kind of fear that makes you want to laugh out loud – when life seems to break its own rules, the way a joke does, and there is no logical reaction left. I shut the door behind me.

But what rules? What rules are you breaking, anyway? I asked myself. Where did this idea of rules come from? From Dad, who had been unfaithful? From Mum, who had been unhappy? Were they something half remembered from those misty first Communion lessons – that bunch of unlikely stories read by fat Mrs Faulkner, with the squinty eye?

I remembered that eye perfectly. It always seemed to be looking past you. And I remembered Sister Julia's hare lip. I thought: why are good, religious people so often hideous? Oh, you be happy, even if it kills you, I told myself.

On the road, a plastic bag, fat with the wind, bounced across the tarmac in front of me. An image of bins spitting rubbish, newspapers slapping against the railings, cans singing in the gutters. The sanctity of marriage, I thought – even the gate laughed as I opened it. The trees were shaking with it.

And then I found that Simon had left the front door open for me, and – as would happen so often in the future – just that small act of tenderness from him, of concern for me, was enough to fill me with love and hope. I pushed the door and its give was almost erotic – a whispered assent. There was furniture stacked in the hall – a lamp, two chairs, a mattress. They must have dismantled that bed, I thought, and felt a flash of superstitious fear. But there was no place for fear any more – he was too close, and I was too hopeful.

'Hello?' I called out. The emptiness was like a cool, blank stare.

'Hey, I'm in here,' Simon called back to me.

He was sitting in the room where I hid the night before. It was full of street light. There was a saucer full of cigarette butts beside him and he was drinking a bottle of beer from a pack in a plastic bag. There were two empty bottles beside him. He smiled.

'I was giving up on you.'

'I was waiting – I didn't know when to come.'

'No.'

He looked as though he had been really frightened. I sat down near him and took one of his cigarettes. He leant over to light it for me and his boots scraped dust up off the floor as he moved. My hand was shaking.

'Are you OK?' he asked me.

'I'm fine.'

'I'm terrified,' he said. 'Where's Tom tonight?'

I shrugged my shoulders.

'Rachel's gone to Edinburgh. New play – she'll be up and down for a month or so.' He pushed his hand through his hair.

'I'm sorry. I'm an idiot. Why talk about it? Jesus.' He put his cigarette out and looked out of the window. His wrists rested on his knees and his head leant back against the wall. I sat quietly and watched him. He looked pale and scared. Just then I felt intense pity for him. I wanted to say I was sorry to have brought him to this, that I could just go and everything could be put back together again. And for a moment, even that thought brought relief – of course I could just go. Be a child. Cry it out. Forget about him.

But the fear that he would agree felt like blood poisoning. I pictured him letting me out, apologising – 'You're a lovely girl . . . I just . . . I'm *married*, for God's sake.'

He turned back to me.

'What do you think, Emily? What are you thinking about all this?'

I smiled, feeling sick, feeling that if I could just kiss him maybe the thinking would stop, the emptiness might shrink between our mouths.

'I don't know,' I said. I was looking at his hands, his bare arms below the rolled shirtsleeves. I could feel them moving against my mouth. He opened another bottle of beer and passed it over to me.

'How did you get yourself mixed up in our family, anyway? Our faithless bloody family. Really, of all the good-looking men who must be interested in you, why Tom?'

'Not Tom – *you*,' I said.

Simon looked down at his hands. For a moment, as he spun the beer fizzing around the bottle, they could have been Tom's hands. He took a long drink and wiped his mouth. I couldn't look at the fear on his face any more. I moved my eyes over the bare walls instead.

'Shit. Just three years ago it would have been . . . but yeah, what's the point of saying it?'

'Look, Simon, I don't want to make you unhappy,' I said.

'Unhappy?' He laughed. 'Emily, you're the most gentle, subtle person I've ever met. You couldn't make me unhappy. I could just watch you – like I watched you at that dinner with your parents.' He smacked his hand against the side of his head. 'I watch you all the time.'

I listened to him – to the words I couldn't have imagined – feeling each emotion run into its opposite with a shower of sparks. Hope that he wanted me ran into despair that he did and now there was no going back. Pity for Rachel ran into hatred, defiance. Then fear ran into peace. I put my hand over his and he looked at me.

'You must know how beautiful you are, Emily, but it isn't even that. It's every little reaction that flicks over your face . . . the way you seem to feel so hard for everyone else; your father, your mother, Andrea – even *me*. It lights you up. All this dull, nerveless cynicism around us, Emily. And now there you are, the bright place in my mind.'

He was so innocent, really. He took a long drink of beer and laughed.

'Jesus, I've never spoken to anyone like this. I didn't even know I was like this – what was in me. God, I've become *ridiculous* –' he screwed his eyes up – 'lying to Rachel about forgetting my wallet, so I could scuttle after you down the road the other day.'

I laughed.

'I'd been spying on you, Simon,' I said, 'hiding behind the bus shelter. I thought you lied for my benefit – poor hysterical girl. You know, to . . . ' I looked down, remembered myself watching them at that café table, holding my breath, 'to preserve my dignity.'

'To preserve *mine*,' he said, 'for what it was ever worth. No, Rachel hadn't seen you and I had to have a reason to go back down the road. I don't even know why I told you – and then you saw the wallet in my pocket – genius that I am. I thought you'd seen through me. I'd never *seen* anyone so desperate to get away.'

'That was to preserve my dignity,' I said. We laughed sadly at the number of misunderstandings in the little knot of circumstances.

The branches of the tree outside slid on the window pane. Then it was quiet. I smelt the wet paint, the damp plaster, the beer on his breath. The warmth had come back into my body.

'Come here,' he told me.

Later we went into the hall and pulled the mattress in. It slapped down in the middle of the floor, sending up a dust cloud into the shaft of street light. It was a pale, bleaching light, which filled the room now the daylight had gone. It slid down our bare arms and legs like cold water; it flashed off his hair when he leant far back with his eyes closed tightly. He made a strange, lost sound. I pulled him down against me to hold on to him and then he was breathing hard against my neck. His hair was soft and dusty in my fingers.

I have never been so still. It was the kind of peace which only comes by contrast. People say happiness is an unthinking condition. All my thoughts fell away unwanted. It was as if my mind became nothing more than a consciousness of the heat of his skin and the weight of his body against me.

My days – I don't even know how many there were – passed in sleep and waiting. At ten, I would walk over to our empty room. Mostly I didn't mind the waiting – the surprise and happiness of finding him sitting there each night, leaning against the wall, was like a slap to my hysteria. My face smarted with happiness all day.

Simon was barely sleeping. An old trouble with insomnia became his ally now. He spent the days working with the builders on the house and the nights with me. He would tell Andrea he was going to bed early and leave her with the papers in the drawing room. He would do his phone call to Rachel. He would slip out to be with me.

I think the more guilt he felt, the more he wanted the house to be beautiful for Andrea. His guilt sanded the floors, dragged sacks of weeds out of the garden, chose a happy, yellow paint for the kitchen.

Time fell to pieces. The day was nothing – morning, afternoon and evening were distant sounds on the street outside, something to do with the flow of traffic. The night was cool and perfect as I closed the door and walked over the road towards him. Then there were the hours we made love, the street light and the dusty mattress.

All normal routine, even mealtimes, had been lost along the way. At around 2 a.m. we would find ourselves starving and Simon would produce crazy ingredients from his backpack. We cooked them in the unfinished kitchen, leaning bowls on cardboard boxes.

Sometimes everything began with one letter. He would bring out pasta, Parmesan, peaches, pecan pie. Sometimes he said things had just leapt into his basket: dark chocolate, croissants, vanilla ice-cream, eggs and cream cheese and sun-dried tomatoes. He would throw things to me – 'You juggle the bananas and I'll whip the cream.'

And he cooked beautifully – what I call beautifully. There were hazardous burnt bits, accidental miracles in which things turned into caramel or rose to crazy proportions. It was an adventure. We picked bits out, tried to guess what ingredient had been forgotten. We would throw things in to see what happened. They were great feasts of strange combinations, and we would sit cross-legged on the floor and eat like hungry children, wiping our mouths on our sleeves, stealing food from each other and laughing. I had never felt so happy.

And at around four in the morning, we would be lying back and talking and the sky in our window would be a brownish purple with the day a white thumbprint behind it, pushing through.

I think the room stopped feeling private about then – when the houses stepped out of the dark, like drab witnesses to what we were doing, stocky and complacent against the sky.

Simon kept a bottle of whisky in his car, to warm us up. At about that time we would walk around for a while, taking sips of it, before anyone woke up. The air was still warm outside – the cold we felt was only the tiredness inside us. We talked about the books we had read and played stupid games: Character in a novel most likely to start a fight at the Christmas party. Best love scene in a play. We chose the same names sometimes and laughed at ourselves or tried to guess what the other one would say. I had never really talked about books with anyone before – except Dad.

After a couple of weeks, we decided on a change of scene and got a taxi out to the Embankment to walk by the river. I had the bottle of whisky sitting in my lap. We slid together on the seat and laughed when the taxi turned the corners. Simon put a cigarette in my mouth and smiled at me while he lit it.

'Happy?' he said.

I smiled back at him.

'I am,' he told me. 'We're going to drink to happiness.'

He touched the bottle in my lap and ran his hand up my leg. His hand was still hot from making love.

The taxi stopped in front of a church and we crossed the road to the river. We leant against the wall. It was a new bottle and Simon pulled the cork out of it.

'Smell that,' he said. 'I thought we should have something delicious.'

There was an excitement about him that night which had made us cry with laughter – he had forgotten the cutlery and we ate spaghetti with our hands. He pulled my hair back tight off my face. 'Look at you,' he said – and then he looked away, along the river. It made me feel sad for a moment.

We drank the whole bottle that time. We followed the river, watching the black water lighten to grey. Lights came on in the office blocks.

An hour or so later, we were laughing and stumbling against each other near Battersea Bridge. The sun was coming up and the early-morning big lorries were on the road, heading out to the motorways. We were comic figures suddenly – drunk before breakfast, out of place in the early-morning people. We stopped on the bridge. Simon held up the bottle and shook the whisky around.

'One last drink each.'

'Use it wisely,' I said.

'We can't use it *wisely*. There are rules. Weren't we

supposed to be drinking to love or happiness, anyway?'

He held the bottle up high and I could see the offices and houses distorted through the glass. I felt unsteady.

'Love or happiness anyway,' he said. He was laughing. The river was beautiful. Nothing held sense any more.

Then he was looking past me. On the ground a little way off, there was a man asleep under a blanket. The way the blanket fell suggested the angles of a bicycle, something mechanical – not the shape of a living man. His head was resting on a pile of plastic bags. The wind moved his hair like long grass. In his arms there was an empty bottle and he held it against his chest, like a child or a lover. Even in sleep, his features held an expression of longing. I recognised that look – it was on my face even when I caught it accidentally in a mirror.

Simon walked over and put the bottle down beside him.

'Let him have it,' he said. 'Everyone should have a bit of what they love.'

We walked back over the bridge. There were gulls standing on the dirty bank. Now and then, one shifted on the mud or flew up and landed again a little way off. By the road, Simon put some money in my hand. A few cars were rushing past now.

'Get a taxi and go to bed and sleep.' He kissed my mouth softly. 'Rachel's back tonight – I can't see you for two days. Will you come on Sunday?'

'OK.'

The quick, clean reproach of her name. His slight hysteria made sense to me now. I looked down at the pavement. For whole hours at a time I forgot her – her neat, smooth face, the sweet smell of her perfume, which sometimes seemed to be on my own hands. She was the cold persistent current beneath everything, threatening to wash away our little mess of happiness. I hated her.

'I'm sorry, Emily,' he said.

I looked up at him, the grey under his eyes, which made his face so gentle.

'It's OK.' I thought how there were no endings between us, really. We had put an end to them the way we had put an end to the gap between day and night. There was just the waiting.

Chapter six

Waiting for Simon. Waiting, under all the slow falling minutes, turning my face up at the sky as if they might suddenly tip down like heavy rain. Sometimes I felt as though waiting was all I did. But really, there was always Tom. My love had changed everything, I thought – days and nights had ended. Maybe nothing is true all the time.

Sometimes, when I was on my own, when I was waiting or when Simon slept far away beside me, then love was smaller than I was. It was an object in my hand. The emptiness of that room failed to hold my imagination and I knew things would have to change soon. Of course they would. The house would be finished, full of Andrea's furniture. Rachel would come back from her play. And I would have to see Tom again.

The impossibility of hiding away from Tom much longer

hung over me. I did not answer his calls. The thought of his face terrified me – as if he had become the image of my conscience. I had not realised guilt would have such bad taste.

The Tom in my mind had his privileged logic. In the night, when I lay with Simon and my thoughts were as soft as my fingers moving on his chest, I would suddenly forget myself and there he was, waiting for me. He raced fast through my memory, tapping his nails on the steering wheel, throwing a cigarette butt out of the window, screeching a U-turn. It hardly mattered that I avoided him physically – he was there in the day, in the lost place my thoughts wandered to. He was just as he had been after that first dinner with my parents, under the hard kitchen lights, with the sad old dishwasher running in the background. He looked as if he had foreseen it all.

After a couple of weeks he left a message on my phone.

'Hi Em – it's me. I'm *guessing* you're alive.'

I felt him behind the light sarcasm. He said he would drop by around seven – and *hope* to see me. 'See you later,' the message ended. Tom dared people to let him down.

I called him back and hung up before the phone rang. My days were punctuated with these half-gestures. Sometimes my mouth would open to speak and then close again with a suppressed rush of breath, making my mother or my sister look round for a second. I would open the front door to go out and then close it again, in my own face, and stand still in the quiet of the hallway.

I opened my bedroom window and leant out. Andrea's car was parked in front of her house. The boot was open and there were boxes beside it, what looked like curtains in a dry-cleaning bag. I saw a lamp sticking out of one of the boxes, a kettle put down on the roof of the car. I felt my mouth go dry. How many boxes could she have? I wondered. I pulled the window down hard.

I could hear Ellie's voice calling me –

'Em? E – *em*?' I could hear her running up the stairs. She pushed open the door. My boots were jammed under it and she struggled for a moment and then kicked them out of the way.

'Em?' she said. She was breathless. She pushed the hair off her face with one of the dramatic gestures that always annoyed my father – 'Piccola Prima Donna,' he called her, pronouncing the words correctly – irritatingly.

'Em? Can I borrow your green shirt? And also have you got any cigarettes?'

I picked the shirt up off the floor and threw it to her.

'It's not clean,' she said.

'No.'

I took the cigarettes out of my pocket and gave her one. She walked over to the window and tugged it up. She frowned hard as she did it, knowing I was watching. I watched her light her cigarette and blow the smoke out carefully into the street. The smoke looked sad coming from her child's mouth.

'Why are you just standing there?' she asked me.

I laughed and needed to do something, so I lit a cigarette too.

'Oh my God, Em – they'll smell it. Get over here.' She pulled me next to her in the window. I tried to fix my eyes on something – anything rather than Andrea's house. Our arms were the same arms. Our hands were the same hands – hers a little rougher, the nails bitten down. I had never really noticed before. I am always surprised by family resemblance – it's as if I thought I had fallen off the moon.

After a while she said what she had come to say.

'Tom said he'd take me out and he never did.'

'Oh Ellie – he's pretty unreliable.'

Her laugh knocked the breath out of you sometimes – she knew what she knew.

'Yeah. Sure,' she said. 'That's just another way of saying he doesn't like me. As a friend, I mean.'

'It isn't.'

'Anyway, I think I'm interested in Sasha's brother now. He's really nice.'

'Is he?'

She looked at me.

'What's the matter? You look so sad.'

'I'm just really tired.'

'But you sleep *all* the time.'

'I know,' I said.

She put the cigarette to her lips again and I watched her try to blow a smoke ring which was just a floppy, little cloud.

'Em?'

'What?' I watched a van move slowly down the road, the radio voice trailing after it.

'Are you OK?'

'Of course I am,' I told her. I smiled, feeling my teeth.

'Is it good being your age? I can't wait till I'm old enough to go out with the boys I like. Everything will be different. I think I'll fall in love.'

She looked at me, to make sure I was really listening. She is someone who wants absolute attention. I looked at the green streaks in her hair.

When she was little she used to need me to sit outside her door when she went to sleep. Every so often, her anxious voice would shout out, 'Are you still there?' I remember once I got bored and went to play in my own room. Ellie tipped her cot over and the side smashed. She cut her hand. Mum had to give her a warm bath to calm her down. I remember her wrapped in her towel, her breath still catching, convulsive. She wouldn't look at me.

'What if it's all just the same when you're my age?' I said. Did I take pleasure in disappointing her? Leave her alone, I told myself.

She took a drag on her cigarette and narrowed her eyes as if this was a distant patch on the horizon which had already worried her.

'It *won't* be the same,' she said. 'And if it is then I'll just kill myself.'

My hand snatched out at her arm. It felt soft and babyish pressed between my fingers. I wanted to tighten my grip. I hated myself.

'Let go, Em. Let go – you're hurting.'

I let go of her and rested my elbows on the windowsill again.

'I won't, then,' she said. 'If you don't want me to. *God.*'

'I don't want you to,' I told her. I felt embarrassed by the strange way I had just behaved, but she didn't seem to care. She was busy, dreaming about herself.

'Well, then I'll be really happy and I'll be rich and have

eight children – all boys. I don't want any daughters.'

I was looking away down the road again. Andrea was laughing back at someone in the doorway. I couldn't see who – her car blocked them out. She took the kettle off the roof of the car and pulled another large box out of the back seat. Then Simon came out and took it from her and they went in.

'D'you want me to go away or something?' Ellie said. She gave me that look of hers – you saw hope trip up behind her eyes. I sat down on my bed and looked at her. I remembered how she told the family counsellor, 'Dad thinks I'm stupid. And I do too.'

She's right: he does think she's stupid. When we were little, I did Latin with Dad and Ellie watched TV. 'Ellie, *scuttle off*, we're working,' he would say. He gave me books for Christmas, Mum chose a jumper for Ellie. Did I enjoy it sometimes? That superiority, the fact I had his attention like no one else. But I always suspected he was making up for Irena, for the times I had waited in the hallway, said nothing to Mum, and the lessons felt dirty.

The cleaning lady made biscuits with Ellie once when Dad and I were doing Latin on the kitchen table.

'Well, you're the *cook* of the family, then,' she told her. 'No one can live off old books, can they?' I could see she felt sorry for her. She scowled in Dad's direction. Ellie made a special big biscuit for me.

I suppose really the unhappiness in our house passed our relationship by. Perhaps it even made us cling together closer against its current. We were conspiratorial. We had a dream about living in a house all alone together. We sat up late in my bed with Dad's torch and drew pictures of it. I used to write 'very good' on her ones. I wanted to make a list of who would be allowed to visit: Mum, Uncle Peter, my friend Nina. But Ellie said no, she wouldn't go unless it was only us. Her eyes went soft and dreamy when she described the rooms. I felt so guilty when I grew out of talking about it, but even now it is still there between us. It is a time that will always have been.

I looked at her pink lipstick, the small breasts under the bright slogan on her T-shirt.

'I can go away if you want,' she said again.

'No, I want you to come here.' She dropped the cigarette out of the window and came over with her head down. I held her against me for a minute, her long hair spread over us, her shoulders hunched down to fit under my arm the way she used to.

'Em? D'you think, when you're really old, you look back and think yes, it was all worth it – all of that was worth it?' she said. Then my mother's voice was calling her. It reached us slowly, the way an alarm clock tears the silk screen of a dream.

'*E*-llie? Sasha on the phone –' and she ran away to get it.

I leant back against the wall and looked out at the perfect blue sky. Every day the sky was perfect that summer. A rich, blue heaven – unreachable.

Compassion, I thought. Is that what you call it? It means nothing. Compassion was just taking a good, luxurious eyeful of a portrait of your own pain. Because when I thought of Tom, I thought of myself. I remembered his stark face looking at me strangely in the bar when I thanked him for a drink. I had kissed his cheek and laughed at something someone else was saying. Laughed in his ear. Hadn't I known what he was asking for? Love? Absolute attention? 'Thank you,' I said. I kissed his cheek – as if he had given me a drink.

And thinking that made me think about myself again. I saw myself walking home after Simon, feeling his warmth snatched off by the early morning air. I smelt the damp leaf smell from the hedges, sensed the white hours ahead. I thought of my picture of Rachel laughing when he met her at the station, the brown arms claiming him back. Was she over there now? I got up and sat back down.

My thoughts of Simon were always these gentle, melancholy sequences, with the knife-wound of her at the end.

I had not seen him for one night. I would see him the next night. There was just tonight to wait out. My teeth made a grating sound and I felt ashamed of myself.

I think I had honestly thought it would be enough to see him from time to time. To pretend I was his. For years I had pretended to be my parents' daughter. I said 'Dad' and I thought of Irena's hallway, the chicken soup smell – the smell of conspiracy against my mother. I said 'Mum' and I thought of her weakness, her slumped shoulders, her eyes closed to pray. In some ways I felt more anger towards her than I did towards my father. She had slammed the door on that au pair girl and cried with relief – that lust, that hissing red mouth was gone. And on Sundays, she arranged the flowers at the church.

I called Tom back and heard the recording of his voice: 'Hi, this is Tom. Leave a message and – I'll get round to it.'

I had nothing to say. I lay down on my bed and closed my eyes.

When I woke up it was ten to seven. The light was thinner now. I looked around my room and thought of Dad asking us something once –

'What would you two save if there was a terrible fire?' He had an expression of detached light amusement on his face: a little fact about his daughters – why not?

'There's not going to be any terrible fire,' my mum said.

'Oh, Jane.'

'I'd take Looby and Snoops and my rosettes,' Ellie said. Dad nodded, slightly bored, at her conventional response and looked at me, eyebrows raised. But nothing – nothing – came into my head. My heart raced, thinking I would hurt him – all those birthday presents he had bought me. Christmas presents. There must be something which meant something to me – something I would save from a *terrible fire*. I thought of all Ellie's treasures, her lock boxes, her shelf of animals. My toys were in the pile the cleaning lady had put them in. Eventually he lost interest in me looking sulkily down at my plate and he moved on.

Nothing pins me down and really I have always been lost for words.

I washed my face and put on clean clothes. I waited and heard Tom's car pull up outside. The music cut out suddenly with the engine. The outside world was heavy with my life now; any sudden ending: a hair-dryer switched off, a lawn mower stalling, could knock the breath out of me. I listened to Tom's shoes scrape up the steps. After I had pictured the anger, the hurt on his face, he rang the bell.

But when I opened the door, it was not Tom, but Jay

standing in front of me. It took a moment for me to understand. The shapes were wrong, the picture was wrong.

'Hi, gorgeous,' he said. He kissed my cheek with his dry lips. 'Tom's in the car. You coming out?'

I felt laughter – anything – welling up inside me to compensate for the anticlimax.

'Out?' I said.

I heard the cars rushing by. It seemed stupid now to think that Tom would have had anything to say to me. It was impossible to believe sometimes that I was the only person who knew what had happened. I thought my love was like a surprise snowfall then. It had fallen softly in the night and made the whole world brighter and clean and so quiet. Surely everyone had opened their curtains on it that morning.

But Tom had not noticed. He knew nothing about it. No one knew anything about it.

I looked down the road towards his car and he waved at me through the windscreen. I smiled and waved back. Perhaps talking to me was beyond him anyway. There had been that time on the kitchen step at Andrea's party, but I had felt safe knowing he would give up if I looked distant enough. His father's absences, his mother's unintelligible laughter had taught him to cover his head over with the safety of himself. So, when he did try to talk to me, I looked as far out into the garden as I could – and Tom tore up mint leaves into little pieces.

'Just be a second,' I told Jay.

In those next few moments something new happened to me. It was between me and my conscience. I ran up the stairs to get my bag. I listened to my feet thudding on the carpet as they had all my life and I felt the weight of apprehension falling away from me. And then suddenly I felt like I could have laughed – maybe I did laugh. I had told myself a happy lie – that Tom's love for me felt nothing like my love for Simon. I packed up all I knew about him, all our similarities – that painful hope of his which I could never escape – into one neat lie.

It was the way Dad must have told himself my mother didn't notice – and just then I wondered why I hadn't done it before.

Why do you always assume other people think like sad old you? I asked myself. Their separateness, which had always made me dream, made me lonely – that was their thick skin, their essential difference. Circumstances bounced off, so there was less of them to know – less chance of hurting. It was only me and Simon who took experience like a blow to the face, like a long kiss. I felt my dirty mouth smiling.

The window was still open in my room. The evening air felt cool and soft and full of potential. It felt the way it used to in queues outside bars when the drinks and the music were new and amazing to me and I thought everything, everything might change tonight. I picked up my keys and my cigarettes. Ellie's music was going quietly in her room – a song she was always playing. What was wrong with that? My sister was playing her favourite song. Soak it all in your melancholy, I told myself. Go on, let everyone drown and choke, and sit there on your own.

No. I loved someone and he loved me and what was the matter with the outside of it being secret and wrong? The inside was more than I had ever had.

'Bye, Ellie,' I called out to her. My voice sounded high and strange. I ran down the stairs and then I got into Tom's car – as if nothing had happened since I last saw him.

We went for supper in the Italian restaurant that Tom liked. I was starving and the food was good there. It was busy that night and the conversations were loud all around us. There was music playing and there were candles and it was a good atmosphere.

Tom spent a lot of money in that place and the waiters treated him like an older man, calling him sir, asking if he would like his usual table. His friends would turn up gradually, expecting to find him at the long table in the corner. We had often stayed until all the chairs were stacked and the floor had been mopped around us. Sometimes Gianni, the owner, would come out with a broom or something, prop his pin-striped elbow on it and pretend to be asleep. We would all laugh and get the picture. Then we would go on to Raf's.

We sat down. Tom ordered two bottles of red wine and the thin waiter gave us a wink.

'A man who does not like to hold back,' he said. He had a thick Italian accent and I guessed he was one of Gianni's nephews. They liked to try out colloquial English on us. He went away for the wine.

'Oh, you'd be surprised,' Tom said quietly.

The waiter came back with the wine and put a basket of olives and bread on the table. He began to uncork the bottle and then he poured a little for Tom to taste. Tom nodded seriously, but the waiter was not really concentrating. He smiled at me.

'Where you been all this time?' he said, 'they miss you in the kitchen.' He jerked his head towards the flaps in the wall where they passed the food through and two of the kitchen helps grinned and waved at me. I laughed.

'We've all missed her,' Tom said. 'Haven't we, Jay?'

Jay looked uncomfortable.

'It's good to see you out again, Em.'

'Look I haven't been ill or anything, you know?' I said. It was starting to annoy me. I do what I want, I thought. Just because they're too insecure to break their routine doesn't mean I have to be. The waiter poured the wine out for us.

'So what's up, then? You becoming a nun?'

The waiter looked at Tom and clutched his chest as if he was heartbroken.

'Non! Ma che peccato,' he said. Then he winked at me again and went away to take another order. I was sorry he had gone. I liked him playing the fool.

'Of course I'm not becoming a nun, Tom.'

'Yeah? Or Jay's given me fifteen to one on you two-timing me.'

'Tom, man,' Jay said.

'Thirty to one it's another girl.'

'Hey Tom,' Jay said, 'I think you *might* be bullshitting.'

Tom laughed. He gave me a cigarette and I lit it and started my wine. His hand stroked my hair and then he pulled me towards him. His voice was whispering.

'Don't disappear for so long, yeah?' he said. He put his fingers under my chin and tilted my face up, smiling hard at it.

'Yeah?'

'No,' I said. I smiled back. In spite of myself my eyes ran

slowly over the soft lips, the childlike wide brown eyes. You couldn't help loving his face and it *meant* nothing. It moved you to pity – excitement, but it was just well balanced, well coloured in.

A few of Tom's friends arrived and Jay stood up and called out to them. My friend Sarah was there. I had not seen her since the night Tom and I had dinner with Tony. I felt still in all the kissing.

'Emily,' Sarah said, 'have you actually *lost* your phone?'

She had left a lot of messages for me.

'I'm sorry,' I told her. 'Come and sit with me?'

She kissed me, then she shook her head at me and sat down on the bench. Feeling her sitting next to me, wearing clothes just like the clothes I was wearing, I wished I had called her back. The sight of the boots we had bought her together made me want to speak to her alone, to tell her everything that had happened. I thought about the day we had bought them – a blustery day – our shopping bags swinging into our legs, our laughter knocked back into our mouths. I had loved making Sarah laugh – she laughed all her ambitiousness out like smoke sometimes and then we were really friends.

She uncrossed her legs and crossed them over the other way and I thought if I don't stop looking at those boots I am going to cry. I laughed along with the rhythm of the others and then I listened to what she was saying.

'She is *such* a bitch, though.' She made a characteristic pause for drama and took a drink from her glass. 'Still, that boyfriend looks like justice.'

'Hey, Dom's OK,' Tom said. He would never hear men criticised. 'He's a bit uptight, that's all.'

'Oh come *on* – she doesn't even *get* any. Suzie told me. Some religious thing. He's not bad looking either – though you don't really notice when you know. Jesus, I'd go *mad* in about half an hour.'

This was part of the myth she liked to perpetuate. One night I had looked after Sarah when she got too drunk. I remember her high heels sliding on the bathroom floor, the short skirt hitched above her knickers.

'I hate it,' she said. 'I just wish they didn't have to *touch* you.'

She turned around and held her glass up at me.

'Cheers, Em – good to see you out again.' The same phrase Jay had used. I wondered how much my absence had been talked about. We drank back our wine together.

The night was quiet when we burst out on to it – eight of us now – heels clicking on the pavements; laughter. We got cabs out to Raf's – two of them. They set off together and we waved and made faces through the window like children, pretending it was a race if ever they pulled up alongside each other.

I had begun to feel drunk and good. My head leant back heavy on the black leather seat and the stars and lights spun in the window. Someone shook my arm.

'Don't bale out on us yet, Em.'

I laughed and straightened myself up.

We seemed to arrive quickly and Tom paid the driver while the rest of us climbed out. I looked at the entrance to Raf's, the smoke and the thud of the music, the narrow staircase down. I felt as though I lived in another country now. My love for Simon, the setting for my new life – a dusty mattress and an empty room – were all my world now. This scene in front of me was a sentence in a letter from home.

The bouncer, Grenville, faked a double-take when he saw me, but he was too busy to talk, dealing with a group of four drunk boys. They were too drunk to need any more. Jay put his arm round my shoulders and whispered to me, 'Got some pretty nice coke earlier.'

He pressed his wallet into my hand. Grenville patted his back as he lifted the cord across the doorway and Jay walked down the stairs ahead of me. Drugs were making Jay everyone's friend. He turned and smiled when we got to the bottom and I thought how threatened he had looked in our garden when I told him I didn't feel like going out any more. There was such relief on his face now. I didn't care. I smiled at him and made my way to the toilets with his wallet.

As I pushed the door open, a girl making a lipstick face in the mirror, lips stretched in a cartoon 'O', let her eyes flick at me. There was a smell of perfume and the hot metal of the hand dryer. The spotlights made round patches of white light on the floor; they flashed off my shoes as I walked through them. Then the cubicle door was shut and locked and I was invisible. I imitated that lipstick face and stuck my tongue out at the door. I felt so much mockery, so much hatred for everything that wasn't Simon. To me there was love and there were the things that threatened it. It had made me a spiteful person. I turned to the side and stuck my tongue out at Tom, who was somewhere two walls along, holding his new drink, his new vulnerability.

I found the wrap in Jay's wallet and cut a line on the cistern, then I took it and went back out. I did not catch myself in the mirror.

When the door swung shut behind me, I looked out at the place where I had spent most of my time with Tom. It didn't matter to me what I saw now – I think I had been afraid to be critical before. Afraid of spoiling it for myself. Now it had nothing to do with me.

The bar was the focal point of the room. It was dark polished wood and above it the bottles flashed against green glass the colour of sea water. There were spiky, metal lamps etching down from the ceiling, like forking lines on a heart-rate monitor. There was hip-hop playing – something Tom would have called 'retro'. Mounted in each corner, just beneath the ceiling, were blank blue computer screens, unblinking eyes. And then, to set it off, because nothing was stated categorically there, all along one wall there was a nineteenth-century tapestry of fat cupids clutching each other's ankles, laughing and flying about in a turquoise sky. Underneath sat people in their twenties, in their beautiful clothes, mouthing in the loud music.

My friends stood along the front of the bar. I walked over to join them and gave Jay his wallet.

'Rocking,' he said. His hand shook as he put the wallet back in his trouser pocket. His feet could not stay still.

'You OK?' I said. He made the sound of a rocket flying through the air. The light hit his eyes for a second. I heard Sarah laughing.

'And the moral of the story is?' she said in a game-show voice. She raised her eyebrows and looked at Jay.

'Didn't hear the story, babe,' he told her.

'Never mind. Make it up. Have a go.'

The others had stopped listening now. She had been funny – they still had smiles on their faces, but she had shut them off, made it clear with the strange brightness in her eyes and voice that they were not needed as an audience for a moment. This was her private, melancholy joke. She made it in a lot of different ways. Once she had asked me to finish all her sentences for her – see what happened. A game of consequences, she said. She wanted to tell people how lonely she was – that she was lonely enough to believe nonsense was all there was in the world. Then she would laugh it off. She did that now. I think she knew I took her seriously and it made her look away from me at those times.

Tom's friend Luke put a drink down in front of her. He was not as bright as she was and she let him make a virtue out of it in a way women still do sometimes – as if he had been allotted her share of common sense.

'Moral of the story? No *mo*rals, Sarah,' he said. 'It's a Friday fucking night.'

He had blond hair which looked pale green in the light, smooth as aluminium. He frightened me. Sarah said she had been in love with him for ever. Jay threw her his wallet and she caught it against her stomach.

'Jesus, I was hoping for something profound – something in Latin or whatever.'

There was some quiet laughter – the laughter of people in a secret society. That was how it had been for all of us at school, anyway. It was a fiction my own friends and I had also maintained to make things more exciting. A them and us fiction. And all it was in reality was the possession of a mixture of class A and B drugs. There was no secret society. That same mixture was in the pocket of every sociable teenager in London. At Raf's, where people were a few years older, childish fictions seemed to have long been discarded. So, Tom's friends were a society beginning to question their allegiances: What holds people together out here? that laugh asked, with its note of uncertainty. There seemed to be no loyalties at all between the shining individuals at the tables, with their dirty, ironical laughs. Sarah went off to the toilets.

I have my loyalty though, I thought. I felt the happiness sting behind my eyes and the tables blurred until I blinked it away for later.

When I turned back to the bar I found Tom looking at me.

'You should come over to the house, Em – see what we're doing to it.'

'Yeah, I'd love to,' I said. I felt my fist clench.

'You seriously won't recognise bits of it – mostly upstairs and the kitchen, downstairs is still a bit of a ghost town. But the builders have done quite a bit. And of course Simon's such a *saint*,' he said. It sounded like an Andrea phrase. He blew his cigarette smoke up in front of his face.

'You've been helping, too, though, haven't you? I mean, I've seen your car sometimes.'

For some reason, this got past without him questioning me.

'I go round from time to time. There's not much for me to do, really. It's not even like I'll be living there for long. Who knows where I'll be in a year's time?' This excited him. His eyes narrowed and he took a drink from his glass. 'Yeah, I could be anywhere. Anyway, Rachel's come up with this whole complicated design scheme. Art deco this, rosewood that – fuck knows. Mum likes it.' He stubbed his cigarette out.

'What's she like?' I said.

'Rachel?' The name had so little significance on his lips. 'She's great.'

It was a word that meant nothing – a worn-through banknote. Had he used it deliberately to leave me empty handed? You win, I thought, hating him. But he knew nothing about my desperation. I felt myself sinking, longing to ask him more.

He took a drink, paused to move an ice cube away from his mouth. I saw his teeth through the glass and then he lowered it and said 'She's kind of neurotic, though.' I listened to him crunching an ice cube slowly, carefully.

This was a standard description from Tom and I knew it, but there was my voice again anyway,

'Neurotic?'

'Yeah. I don't know – she's always having these migraines and she doesn't eat anything and shit. I think she's quite a hassle for Simon. Sexy, though – yeah, definitely sexy.'

I wanted to throw my drink in his face. I saw his father in him – that slow, satisfied stare up the legs, over the breasts. I saw my own father – his dilated eyes watching Irena's hand stroke my face – when we all knew where her hand would rather be.

'But it's weird talking about her like that, though. I mean they're married and shit.'

'She can still be attractive, can't she?'

'Off the market, though – takes away the sex appeal, really. There has to be a chance, doesn't there?'

'Marriages don't necessarily last for ever. She hasn't disappeared just because she married him.'

My phrasing was wrong. I felt the intimacy of 'him' like a pinch on my arm – 'just because she married *him*'. I should not have assumed the name – even though I breathed it in and out all day. Suddenly Tom looked angry.

'Are you suggesting I should fantasise about my cousin's wife?'

For a moment I felt frightened. But he was just angry at my lack of jealousy. It had always annoyed him.

'No,' I said. 'Don't be stupid. Have another drink.'

When Sarah came back from the toilets, I pulled her away to dance. We went right into the middle of the dance floor and I closed my eyes to feel the drug working on my blood. I was less drunk now, but the alcohol always caught up in a while. Every so often, I glanced over at the bar and I saw Tom talking, silhouetted against the shiny bottles.

He had become the man of opposites – playing a card game with my most secret thoughts, laying down one card of sorrow for each one I laid down in happiness, one of anger for each one I laid down in peace. I hated him.

We danced until I felt the sweat running down my back. Sarah danced beautifully – she only did what she was good at – and I liked to watch her. I tied my hair up, feeling the sweat cool and dry on my neck. But the place was crowded, each breath seemed to have steam in it. I wanted a glass of cold water.

Tom was still at the bar. I would have to go up to it beside him. The need for water was too strong –

'Getting a drink,' I told Sarah – but she didn't hear. The

heat was suddenly incredible and I felt panic as I made my way through the crowd. I felt my tongue stick to the roof of my dry mouth.

I leant across the bar and asked for the water.

'Jesus, look at you,' Tom said. 'It's supposed to be fun, you know.'

The water arrived and I knocked it back, too fast to swallow. I felt the ice knocking against my teeth. I drank in long gulps, my eyes closing with each one, and I felt a cold stream of water curl down my neck. I felt it collect in a little pool above my collarbone. Then Tom leant over very slowly and I felt his tongue touch my neck where the water was. I pulled away from him.

'Let's just go,' he said quietly. The blood had drained out of his voice.

'Why? No. Let's stay – I want to dance some more. Jay, you'll dance with me,' I said. I put my hand out and gripped his arm.

'Definitely, babe,' he said. He held up his glass full of green poison in the bar light. 'Just finish my drink.'

I felt sick.

'I'll drive you home,' Tom said.

We caught a taxi back to his car in silence. I watched his hands all the way, rolling and unrolling a £20 note. Then he was handing it to the driver and the door was open in front of me, the pavement like the end of a tunnel ahead.

We walked towards his car and he unlocked the doors with a clean thud. I looked at him. I had nothing to say.

'Jump in, then,' he said. And then he smiled at me. It was

a kind smile and I felt fear and confusion turn my stomach again.

We drove out past the river as we always did, and I thought of those hours I had spent there with Simon, drinking whisky, the dark sky lifting off above our laughter. I remembered Simon's face staring at me, like a pointed gun:

'Look at you,' he said, for no reason. And then he looked away, along the river – as if he had thought better of something and dropped the gun down into the water.

The car pulled up with a jolt.

'Emily? What the fuck's wrong?' Tom said.

I looked back at him. His face was so young looking. I imagined all the school plays, the sports days his exotic parents had never made it to.

'I'm OK,' I said.

'Are you having some kind of a breakdown?'

'What?' I felt tears run over my chin. I wiped them away with the back of my hand and smiled at him.

'No. I'm OK. But you should take me home.'

He started the car again and we drove the short distance back to my house.

There was no avoiding a confrontation of some kind now. The car turned into the top of my road and I thought about all the times we had done this before. Tom's hand would be up my skirt by now, his nails pressed against my thigh. He always stopped under the large tree at the end of the road, where the street light was blocked and we were in near darkness. He would unbutton his trousers, tell me what he wanted, pull me on top of him, his fingers bruising my wrist. He would push me back over into the passenger seat and follow, pressing me back against the car door, crushing my face against the window. There were patches of my hot breath and saliva on the glass when it was finished.

'Let me out,' I said. I could feel my heart going. His eyebrows contracted very slightly and then he stopped the car.

'No,' he said. He turned his beautiful face on me.

'I want to get out.' I knew the door was open, but I didn't move. He did that to me. I waited.

'No,' he said. 'You can't go.'

He switched off the engine and looked out, his face lit up like a Greek sculpture in the street light.

'Have you got any cigarettes?' he asked me. I gave him one. I watched the match and jumped when he struck it. I could not swallow.

'Do you not trust me or something, Em? Is that it? Do you think I'll fuck around or something?' He shook his head at the street, arguing with himself. 'Because I won't. I don't believe in that shit, Emily. I've seen it fuck up my family. I believe in *one* person. *One* person – for ever. Never looking at another person until you *die*. Fuck divorce statistics – *fuck* them. I believe in you go into a church and you stand in front of God and everyone you care about and you say "I promise". *For ever.*' He brought his palm down – slap – on the steering wheel and then he sighed. 'And that's a promise which can never break. Not really.'

He amazed me. I couldn't think of anything to say.

'Do you believe in that, Emily?' He waited for me to speak and then he looked at me.

'I don't know,' I said.

'Because I'm not like my dad. I'm *not.*' He put his hand on my leg – softly. It felt warm. I looked out at the pavement, a fence throwing bars of shadow across it –

'I don't love you,' I said. 'I'm sorry.'

For a moment he didn't say anything and the hand stayed there, deadweight. For some reason I thought about the sister he had never mentioned, I wondered what she looked like. I had forgotten her name and I wanted to ask him.

'Just go home, then,' he told me.

I opened the door and got out. I stood on the pavement as he drove away.

The stars were beautiful and cold on the eye and I felt for the keys in my pocket.

Chapter seven

Sometimes the world seems to offer up an unexpected kindness. Who knows where it comes from, but you take it and you don't question why it's happened. As I walked up the stairs to my room, I saw there was a message on my mobile. It was Simon. Rachel had caught the overnight train rather than the early-morning one the next day, and he had hoped to speak to me. He was just saying good night, he said. I listened to the message again, to hear the gentle disappointment in his voice.

The music had been too loud at Raf's to hear my phone ringing. It had sat unnoticed in my bag – the only thing I had wanted to hear. My love was too gentle and quiet for a stupid, loud place like that.

I called him back. His voice was sleepy – I could feel the

warmth of him, remember his weight in my arms. I wondered how I would contain the fear in my voice.

'Em?' he said.

'Simon, I'm sorry. It's – God, it's *half two* in the morning. I'm really sorry.'

I listened to him turning over in his bed – imagined the sheet sliding over his legs.

'Are you OK? Is everything OK?' he said.

'Simon, please come over.'

Say it simply, I told myself. Say the simple truth.

'Look I'd just really love to see you. Come and stay in my room.'

There was a second's pause, while he took my words in. I had never asked anything of him before – he had just waited for me, with the door propped open, knowing I would come. He cleared his throat. I sensed him shaking the sleep away from him.

'Oh, Em – it's really risky,' he said – and his words smacked into their echo, always waiting in my mind.

Then I thought of Tom's hand on my leg, that small dead-weight of all his disappointment –

'Please,' I said. 'Everyone's asleep here. I'll set an alarm and you can leave before they get up. Simon, I just want us to lie in a proper bed together.'

He thought for a moment and then he told me he would be there in twenty minutes.

Tom had never even been into my room. No one had ever slept in my bed with me before. I had always thought that was why it was so quiet in there. It felt far away, unfingerprinted. I had always kept my bed crisp and clean and white –

Oh, you stupid, prissy little girl, I thought.

For the first time I saw how sex in club toilets, parked cars, spare bedrooms with the party thumping through, had been my own sad private joke – just as Sarah had hers. A parody of intimacy since adolescence, designed to leave me empty hearted, proved right all along. What a theory I had begun with.

Now all I wanted was to lie with Simon breathing beside me, feel his warm chest and shoulders take up all that room I had been so clean and lonely in.

I thought about our first night together, lying naked on the mattress, talking, smoking. Simon had stared out of the window and shrugged –

'Because what is there?' he said. 'What do we move around for, really? Love. Always love.' He had seemed so much older than me then, so much better travelled.

And the fact that 'Love. Always love' – my newly acquired wisdom – had led to that terrible scene with Tom just moments before? Love hadn't done that. I had. It was just the last pulse of static from my old confused life, the last of what I had locked outside my bedroom door. Simon had brought the simplicity I had always needed – there was no questioning the sharp pain of loving him. I sat down on the edge of my bed and folded my hands in my lap. The longing I felt to see him then was like the clean smack of a doctor's hand to a newborn child.

In fact, in spite of everything, there had been simplicity between us from the moment we met. I remembered looking at him against the sunny window in the drawing room when he came for dinner with my parents, and how we had both laughed together – at nothing at all. There was *always* laughter between us – a shared sense of brute comedy muscling in on all our good intentions. It needed no explanation. I smiled, thinking about it. It was that sense which had been between us the time he saw me crying and followed me, leaving Rachel at the café, explaining he had left his wallet in the car. I had pointed at it sitting right there in his shirt pocket and his eyes closed and he sat down and smiled at me. There was such generosity, such humility in his smile. He had looked over at me once, on the step in Andrea's garden –

'Always laughing,' he said. No one had ever thought that of me before. Maybe I had fallen in love with this new, laughing self a little, when I fell in love with him.

His love for other people was simple too. He was *simply* grateful. He didn't corrode his gratitude with questioning how much Andrea relied on him. She had taken him and Rachel in until they had enough money for a place of their own – and he was grateful to her. And he meant to express his simple gratitude by doing work on her house.

'Andrea's an amazing woman,' he said – because she had survived a lot of disappointment. That was *true*. He didn't judge, he had compassion, he made me see what was true.

It makes me smile sadly now to remember the truths my mind did not run over again and again. I did not think about Rachel then, or about that first 'simplicity' of Simon's which I had fallen in love with over the supper table at home:

'And then I met Rachel and there was that whole thing with her going into hospital and I knew love wasn't about *re*trospect or pre*dic*tions or any kind of thinking at all. I just sat by her bed.'

When he arrived, I closed the front door softly and led him silently up the stairs. We passed my parents' bedroom and then the spare room, where my father was snoring. The house felt solid and full of sleep. It felt ordinary. We went up to the top floor where Ellie and I have our rooms. I shut my bedroom door and turned round. Simon looked at me sadly and held my face in his hands.

'My poor Emily,' he said. I felt the weak tears which he could always bring out of me. He kissed me softly and then much harder. Our clothes came away from us like dead leaves.

My mother had been in and closed my curtains and the room was in warm darkness. I smelt my own smell on my own sheets as we lay down. I stared over his shoulder into the dark. This was not like making love on the dusty mattress, in the bright, hard street light. There were so many dreams to drift away on there. That room was an empty frame for dreaming to fill. This was a warm house, my childhood house. I could hear the old hot water pipes next door hissing between our breaths.

'I love you,' I whispered some time later, 'I love you' – and then came the strange, lost sound.

For a long time he lay half across me, his hot arm over my neck, his heart going hard into my left shoulder.

'You're all right aren't you, Em?' he said. His voice sounded cracked with exhaustion.

'I'm OK,' I told him. 'I love you.'

He stroked my hair away from my eyes and I felt him

settle heavily into his pillow. The weight of an incredible tiredness hovered over me. Tom would forget about me. He would find some other girl who would laugh and dance with him. A girl in sharper focus, who would not disappear beside him into her own loneliness the way he disappeared into his. An invisible couple. Tom would forget about me – and Simon is asleep in my bed, I thought.

And then I fell asleep too. For the first time, after nights of watching him like an anxious child – as if he might put the book down softly, turn the light out, betray me, if I closed my eyes – I fell asleep beside Simon with a feeling of perfect safety.

We woke up to the sound of my phone ringing. My sleep had been so deep I was afraid it had been ringing for hours. I glanced at the clock. It said four and I wondered for a second if it could be four in the afternoon – but I had set an alarm for Simon at 6 a.m.

I answered the call.

'Em? Em?' the voice said. It was Sarah. There was fast talking around her – rustling, footsteps. She held the phone away from her mouth and shouted to someone,

'*Now*. I'm coming *now*.'

I could hear her heels walking fast on the pavement. Her breath jolted with each step.

'Em?'

'I'm here, Sarah.'

'Em – there's been an accident. Tom's crashed his car.' She was crying. Her voice sounded weak and frightened. I felt Simon sit up beside me.

'There was an *ambulance,* Em. They've gone in an *ambulance for fuck's sake,'* she said.

She started to cry again and for a moment I just listened to the sounds she was making. I felt my new peace free-falling away from me – and now there was only hate instead. I pieced together what must have happened – he had gone back to Raf's, got wasted, tried to drive on somewhere else. He could never let the night end quietly.

I felt no pity for Tom in his ambulance, or for my friend crying on the phone. I was full of anger and cold poison – as if this had been his winning move and she was reporting it with all the complacency of the morning light which ended my times with Simon. I thought about how quietly Simon and I had come up the stairs, and the brutal publicity of what Tom had done – as if it had been done to hurt me. I thought about the fear in Sarah's voice – the incredulous little rich girl, I thought. You could hear her faith in the world – her parents' money, the private health care in the drawer in the study – straining against this violent surprise in front of her. She was almost unable to say the word 'ambulance', was she? It seemed to blend so naturally into that lifelong ringing in my ears.

'Are you still there, Em?'

'I'm here,' I said.

'Oh my God, it's been so terrible. Jay had *blood* on his face, Em. They put him on a stretcher. He had all this fucking *blood* on him.'

She took a deep breath.

'Fuck, I'm sorry, Em. It's the shock. I mean it's even *worse* for *you* and I'm just blubbing down the phone at you. It's just the shock. I'm trying to keep it together – I really am. We're all fucked, though. You know how it was. My head's not fucking straight and it's like no one knows what to say or do.'

I heard her shutting a car door and the background noise was cut out, the atmosphere suddenly tight around her.

'Which one, Sarah – which hospital?'

She told me the name and I said I would see her there. I hung up.

I told Simon what had happened and we got dressed and went down to his car. The sound of the front door shutting behind us frightened me. Suddenly I wished I had woken my mother and told her. I thought of her sleeping face, the book by her bed, the jars of cream and photographs laid out on her dressing table. They were all photographs of us when we were little. There was a grainy one of Ellie on my lap – the flash and Mum's face in the mirror behind us. I remembered how we used to get into bed with her early on Sunday mornings sometimes.

Why did I feel so much anger towards her? She was just disappointed in love and doing the best she could – like Tony, like Andrea, like my father – like me. But I had started that way. What hope is there for you if you start out disappointed in love?

When Simon started the car, the engine was so loud I pictured white shatter lines forking along the air. We drove off without talking. Once, he put his hand on my arm, but he took it off to change gears and he didn't put it back again. The roads were empty and dirty and the air was sour tasting with fumes.

He pulled up outside the hospital. It was a tall block building spattered neon bright. In the car park were a few cars which threw long, distorted shadows over the tarmac. We did not look at each other as I unbuckled my seat belt. There were just the mechanical noises – the handbrake, the seat belt buckle, the hazard lights –

'Look, I'll call Andrea if he's been hurt,' I told him.

'OK. Good. He might not be hurt, though. He might not be.'

'No.'

We looked at each other for a moment –

'You should go in,' he said. 'You'll call me, too?'

I nodded and shut the door. It was not in either of us to kiss each other goodbye.

I walked across the tarmac towards the bright entranceway to Casualty. There was a warm wind blowing, it rustled in the bins. A wiry dog trotted past me and sniffed a car wheel. It was a lonely place. A light on was an emergency.

The waiting room felt like the bottom of the sea, full of shipwrecked figures. It was the deepest point of the building, heavy with all the rooms above it. It vibrated with stored electricity, with waiting. The picture looked badly conceived – dishevelled figures against the clean floors, the ordered seating. Even the smell was an accident played out in the air – an unhappy marriage of beer and disinfectant. Shoes scraped on the plastic floor. A deep, liberated smoker's cough bristled out from the corner. There were muffled phones, the click of a computer keyboard.

The receptionist was plump. She had a bag of biscuits by

her computer. She brushed the crumbs off her front and smiled at me, waiting for my question.

'All right beautiful?' someone called. The words passed along with him. It was a rich, Hispanic voice. A singing voice. She looked round and rolled her eyes at a porter pushing a trolley – whistling now, down the white hallway. Their happiness seemed staged, unintelligible, pushing shoots between the accidents, the blank stares.

'Can I help you?' she asked me. She let her smile fade tactfully. I explained who I had come to see. She made a phone call and told me where the others were waiting. I went up alone in the lift.

The waiting room my friends were in was three floors up. Sarah was standing in the hallway near the lifts, looking out of an open window. She came over and hugged me when she saw me. She gripped my arm, almost shaking me.

'Tom's OK,' she said. 'He's OK. He's fractured his arm – that's all.'

I felt tears come into my eyes. Her hand stroked my arm again.

'He's OK, Em. He's OK.' She put her arms round me. 'My God, you must have been so scared,' she whispered. I let my eyes close.

'How did you get here?'

'Taxi,' I told her – still able to lie. Yes, still able to lie.

'Poor you – on your own.'

We hugged each other again and this time I was as glad to feel her weight against me as I had been to feel Simon's a few hours earlier. I felt relief – incredible relief, but I knew it was only for myself. To see Tom hurt on a hospital bed would have been facing an image of my own guilt, constructed by a greater artist. I had escaped my conscience for a while. At the last minute, the convicting evidence had been deemed inadmissible – and I had got away with it. I received my hug.

Sarah let go of me softly

'Listen, we don't know about Jay, though. Tom had this box of records on his back seat – it slammed into his head. They think he might be bleeding in his *head,* Em. They kept shining this little torch at him, saying "Squeeze my hand. Can you squeeze my hand, James?" He's having some kind of a scan. We'll find out.'

Jay's records – his fashionable drug-taking, DJ persona, constructed with such attention to detail, his desperate efforts to fit in – had slammed into the back of his head. I thought of the sound he had made a few hours before when I asked if he was all right – a rocket shooting through the air. He had needed to be slowed down – the collision was coming. My heart ached with responsibility – things I could have said:

'Are you unhappy, Jay?' I could have said that. I could at least have said that.

I hurt people. I did nothing.

But this was all an accident! I could not hold myself responsible for the unexpected phone call in the middle of the night. These were the incidental facts of other people's lives and they had left fingerprints all over me. Jay was not *me,* Tom was not *me*. None of this was me and Simon.

Why had I not felt able to kiss Simon goodbye? Fingerprints – making everything dirty. Not so long ago, before Simon, before Tom, what had happened to other people was no more than the tick of a clock in another room. I wanted life to stop meaning again. I wanted my clean bed, our sitting room with the cars going past, saying 'sshh'.

'We just don't know what's going to happen yet. He looked terrible,' Sarah said. 'His mum's in there, waiting.' She glanced at the open window and then down the hall.

'Look, I can't go back in yet. I've got to have a cigarette,' she said. 'Calm me down a bit.'

She took a crushed packet out of her bag. We leant out of the window together and I remembered doing the same thing with Ellie earlier that day. Sarah offered me one and I shook my head.

'I've got to,' she told me – guilty to be indulging herself.

She described what had happened – that Tom had driven into the side of the roundabout a few roads along from Raf's. She was amazed he had been able to start the car. Grenville, the bouncer, had been buying cigarettes and seen it happen. The car flipped *right* over, he said. The paint scraped hard on to the tarmac as it skidded on its roof. It left a line like a silver brush mark along the road. Grenville kept saying it – 'flipped right over, *right* over,' tumbling his hands to show them how – until Luke told him to shut up.

There was a complex of buildings and trees beyond us over a courtyard. I stared out at it. The leaves looked greasy and unnatural in the sodium lights. Growing things looked alien in the twenty-four-hour world. All the bright lights made a starless brown patch out of the sky above us.

'Tom'll lose his licence, you know. He was so wasted,' she said. 'I've never seen him drink like that. We thought he'd gone back with you.' She looked at me questioningly, but her attention wouldn't rest on anything for long. She turned away again.

'His parents'll have to know. Not that any of that shit matters really, but . . .' she blew smoke out in a jet over the empty courtyard –

'I've known Tom since I was little, you know? Have you met his parents?'

I nodded.

'They're really hard on him, I think. I don't know. They think he's a waster. It's not fair to let your child know you think that.'

'No, it's not.'

'It's so hard for him. They're just like this family of super-achievers. His sister's some kind of a *genius*. She speaks Chinese and Russian and shit. They used to play them off against each other all the time. Swimming competitions, word games – chess. I think that's terrible. It's no wonder they don't get on.' She looked down at the cigarette in her fingers and tapped imaginary ash off the end of it – cleaning up. I wondered if she was thinking about her own sister – better looking than her – who had got married and moved to Germany, lost touch.

'And there's this cousin, Simon, have you met him? You'd think *he* was their son, not Tom. Tom absolutely *hates* him. He's a journalist – had some incredible job at *The Times* – New York correspondent or something. He was like the youngest person to ever get the job and Andrea's always banging on about him. It's really unfair – some people just take longer to work out what they want to do, don't they?'

I knew she would never have applied these gentle standards

to herself. I could smell the alcohol on her, the fear.

'But it was so great though, Em, because last year, the incredible cousin – Simon – chucked his in*cred*ible job in. Shocked them all. Tom told me. He suddenly wanted to be like a *teacher* or something – some romantic bullshit it sounded like.' She laughed through her nose,

'Shit, I'm a cynic – maybe he's just the most generous souled person ever. I don't know – I feel spiteful.'

I didn't know either. Simon didn't like to talk about his life to me. We talked about the next ten minutes, the next half-hour – and already what we had done together spanned years of consequences. I looked out, sickened, at the leaves shining in the bright light, against the black sky. The image made a primitive fear in my stomach. I felt the wrongness of the way I had lived those past few months as if I had gone against nature. I had been awake all night, asleep all day. That whole summertime had passed unnoticed, unwanted – adored sometimes into strange distortions. I had remade night and day to suit my purpose, sent time crazy. But just then, looking back, I could see the illusion was thin – that great mass of unwanted minutes had settled in my conscience all along. I felt them suddenly – there in the casualty department, where the lights were on twenty-four hours a day.

'Have you met him then – Simon? He's living with them, isn't he?' Sarah said.

'Yeah, I've met him,' I told her.

'I bet he's an arrogant bastard.' She narrowed her eyes and threw her cigarette out of the window. 'Andrea's got this picture of him winning some rowing thing – grinning. Like a prize bull. I *hate* people who get things too easily. It makes them cruel, I think.'

It was true that the certificates, the rosettes still hanging on Sarah's wall had all been worked for. She had studied night and day for her exams. I had fallen asleep on my desk, been sent out. Had I got things too easily? Was *I* cruel?

'I'm sorry, Em. I'm talking shit. I just need to talk shit for a while.' She smiled at me and I smiled back, liking her – wishing I could tell her everything, but knowing it was impossible now. Her sexual insecurity had always made her far more loyal to men than to women. She had made Tom into her brother overnight, found a subject for all those reserves of pity she would never have spent on herself.

'Shall we go in?' I said. 'They might have heard something about Jay.'

'Yeah, OK.'

The waiting room was long and narrow with a strip of hard-wearing carpet down the middle. A little child had been in there recently – a pile of toys were scattered in the corner and two chairs had been leant together for it to crawl between. Those people had gone now.

Luke and Ronnie were sitting in silence. There was a poster above them of an arm and a hypodermic needle. It seemed like spite to put any kind of a warning in this room. Ronnie's head blocked out the wording and the veined, white hand pointed at his head in limp judgement. A few chairs along was an older woman and a boy of about eight. She looked up anxiously as we came through the door and then her eyes fell away from us and closed softly.

'That's Mrs Lachasse, Jay's mum – and his little brother,'

Sarah whispered to me. We sat down with Luke and Ronnie. I looked at the rosary shining in Mrs Lachasse's lap – her pale fingers moved over it gently. Jay's little brother stood beside her. The features which made Jay look fragile and slightly exotic were heavier on him, more serious looking. He wore glasses pressed right back on his nose, his pyjama top stuck out of his jumper. He was a gaunt little intellectual disturbed in the night – a philosopher, who refused to sit down when his mother patted the seat.

I hadn't known Jay had a little brother. I knew his father was dead. His father had been English, his mother was French. His father had died of cancer. I had never even taken the trouble to picture his mother. And now here she was in front of me, with her thin white arms in her lap, with her little son. Her face was a still surface over all her fear – it twitched out electrically on her rosary now and then.

I felt unsafe. Who knew what happened to people, I thought? Who kept track of the details? She still wore her engagement ring, I noticed. I felt my heart going. What was it like to lose your husband – to be left with two children in a foreign country? What had she done that night? Eaten supper alone, kissed her little boy's head – glanced at the clock, maybe, wondering where Jay was. Avoided the old photographs.

I looked at Jay's little brother. He was still standing, vigilant. His eyes closed slowly and then jerked open as he clenched his fist. His will frightened me. Mrs Lachasse patted the seat again.

'Ma*ma*,' he said softly, patiently. She stroked his hair and then smiled gently and let him be. Maybe that will of his was important to her.

Then I remembered something we had learnt at Sunday school. I heard Mrs Faulkner's voice read it aloud, sing-song for children:

'"Even the *hairs* on your *head* are *all* counted. You are of *more* value than *many* sparrows." That means God loves and values us *all*,' she explained. She looked around, pointing and smiling at each one of us. 'That means He loves *you* and *you* and *you* and *you*.' My eyes closed hearing it again. I thought of all the lights in the hospital.

Shut up now, I told myself. I looked at the clock – it was 5.30. A sense that we should all be in bed, quieter, younger again, made my eyes feel heavy.

Finally the door opened efficiently and a doctor came in. Tom was behind her. His arm was in plaster and his eyes were red from crying or alcohol. Sarah whispered 'Tom', but none of us moved – he seemed to have some serious purpose which blocked us out. He looked at us quickly and nodded and then he sat down beside Mrs Lachasse. She did not look up at him. I saw her hand tighten in her lap. Jay's little brother stared with his dry little face.

'Mrs Lachasse?' the doctor said. She looked up.

'You don't speak much English?'

'No.'

The doctor spoke to her in questions, mothering her confusion for her –

'I'd like to explain about your son, James? Tom will help you understand – my French isn't very good.' She smiled and shrugged apologetically and gestured towards the doorway.

'Shall we go somewhere private?'

Mrs Lachasse nodded and stood up. She still did not acknowledge Tom. Her back was perfectly straight, her little boy was perfectly straight. Tom followed them, looking crooked –

'Estelle . . .' I heard him say as the doctor shut the door behind them.

It was silent again, except for Luke, who was chewing gum.

'She can't speak *Eng*lish?' Luke said. 'Fuck.'

'Jay does everything for her since his dad died. She can't even go to the supermarket without him,' Sarah said. Then her chair scraped on the floor.

'Jesus, though – why can't they say it in here? How long do *we* have to wait?'

'It's the family – they always do the family first,' Ronnie told her. Tom had told me Ronnie's elder brother had AIDS.

'Shit, it's lucky Tom speaks French,' Ronnie said.

Perfect, I thought. Tom – with his capacity to explain himself in so many languages.

After a while they came back. Mrs Lachasse sat down neatly again, her shoulders shaking a little, a tissue in her hand. Her little boy sat curled in her lap, a real child now, his head against her chest.

'Estelle . . .' Tom said again, '*Estelle, si vous le permettez, j'aimerais tout expliquer à ses amis.*' She looked over at us as if from a long way off and nodded.

'He's unconscious at the moment,' Tom said. 'He's fractured his arm, the whole of his right leg and his . . . his eye-socket. Also, he's fractured two of his neck vertebrae and he's going to need an operation.' He swallowed, as if he might be sick, and glanced at Mrs Lachasse. 'They thought he might have internal bleeding, but he doesn't.'

The words she could understand – the list of the broken parts of her son's body – made Jay's mother cry again. She cried openly now.

'Pourquoi?' she said to Tom. *'Que persais – tu être en train de faire? C'était la vie de mon fils que tu mettais en peril. Sa* vie.' She looked at him and he met her eyes sadly, half of himself.

'Drunk,' she hissed – the word dirtier to her in a foreign language. Jay's little brother held on to her tightly.

There was no point in my staying. There would be a long wait and we were not family anyway. I said goodbye and Sarah said she would call me later. I expected she would leave soon, too, but she was not ready yet. I walked out into the bright corridor. The cold blue daylight picked out the ripples in the plastic floor.

So Jay had not been wearing his seat belt, I thought. He had got into a car with his drunk friend and driven off at high speed without putting on his seat belt. Tom had done what harm he could, but as usual, Jay had found a way to take his harm neater, straighter, uncut.

There are some people who carry a special vulnerability around with them all their lives. We had all sensed this in Jay – we let him get away with things that would have been mocked in other people – his clothes, his DJ posture, his over-fashionable lingo. There were sad endings in the shadows under his eyes and we laughed hard at his bad jokes to prove we hadn't noticed.

Outside it was light now. I sat down on the kerb by the entrance to the hospital. The birds were singing, but they were sarcastic birds and it was a wild-eyed, insomniac daylight. It was that time of the morning when the drink wears off and you realise just how thin that little starry black cover actually was. I lit a cigarette and looked around – for what? I felt paranoid.

Everything I had seemed broken, makeshift in that light. I thought about Rachel and Simon together at Andrea's party. They were under a tree, talking to an old lady. It was a snapshot I carried of a tall, perfect, elegant couple. They moved together, their gestures attuned – he leant forward to fill the old lady's glass, she leant back to laugh. In my picture, the sunlight spun off her necklace, it bounced off his glass right at my eye.

I saw her hand showing me its ring –

'He looked all over for just the right thing,' she told me. 'After all – I'll be wearing it the rest of my life.' And then came her laugh – her beautiful, liquid laugh.

It was impossible to see her words as anything other than a warning now. But what could she possibly have seen between us at that point?

'Yeah, little things are always visible to me,' she said. I felt fear – pure physical fear – and I pulled my knees up to my chest. There was no escaping other people. There were no secrets, really. Maybe things are so much simpler than we think: there's telling the truth and there's lying. And there are a thousand tiny ways of lying. In our bright laughter, our casual hellos, Simon and I had already been trying them then.

I saw Rachel's hand with the hard, glinting diamond. I saw Andrea's hand with the soft white circle of skin –

'It doesn't have to end in that,' Simon had said, looking down at it, shocked.

'I don't think it does,' I told him – bowling all of my childish faith right at him. And he smiled at me, grateful – beginning to fall in love.

Chapter eight

I got the bus home from the hospital and managed to get into my room without anyone seeing me. With the sheets pulled over my head, I fell into a blank sleep. I woke up in the late afternoon feeling left behind, my bed grown over with long reeds of yellow sunlight. My father was calling me and I pulled on my jeans and a T-shirt and leant out of the door to hear him.

'Emily?' he shouted, 'You've got a *visitor*' – always a faint sarcasm, no matter what he said. My nerves felt raw and I stood still for a moment and heard his voice carry on below, the witty, plummeting sound of each sentence playing out his sense of fate. It was like a wasp banging into glass. A quieter, woman's voice said something back to him – I couldn't make out the words. The front door closed. They both laughed at something and the sound echoed up from the hallway.

'It's always the way – *al*ways the way,' my father's voice went on. Then:

'Oh for goodness' *sake,* where *is* that girl? I'm so sorry. *Em – i – ly*?' he shouted again.

'*Com*ing,' I called back – fear, anger flashing through the word at him.

I looked at my tired face in the mirror, my red eyes. My hair looked dirty. I walked down the stairs in my bare feet.

Andrea was sitting alone in the drawing room in view of the doorway. My father had gone back to his study. She was looking up behind her at the bookshelves. She looked elegant, draped in her long skirt, sunglasses holding back her hair. She saw me in the corner of her eye and waited a beat before she turned her face towards me.

'Hi, Emily. Sorry this is a bit unexpected, but I wanted a chat,' she said. 'Is that OK?'

I nodded.

'Sure.'

'In here all right?'

'Perfect,' I said. The word was too taut – it showed my nerves.

I went in and shut the door. I sat on the arm of the sofa. My leg shook and I moved it.

'This is such a nice room, isn't it? *Airy,*' she said, 'don't you think?' Her voice was oily and frightening. I looked around me, as if I hadn't seen our sitting room before. I didn't say anything, though.

'Oh look, Emily, I know about Tom, if that's what you're worried about. He could hardly *hide* it from me.'

'No,' I said.

'He came in about nine this morning, shattered. *Frac*tured.'

I looked at her. She liked her wordplay – there was something self-dramatising in everything she said. It diminished her. I sat down properly on the sofa. There was a long silence and I watched her straighten the bracelets on her arm – they jangled brassily.

'Is he feeling OK?' I said – to say something. She smiled.

'You tell me.'

'Well, I only saw him briefly at the hospital. He was busy translating for—'

'That's not what I mean and you know it.'

I looked away at my peaceful window. Her voice changed.

'So what are your plans then, Emily? I feel I hardly know you. What are you going to do with yourself – after the summer?'

'I'm going to university.'

'Really? You must be excited.'

'I'm looking forward to it.' In fact, I had hardly thought about it since the letter of acceptance. I remembered the books on the hall table, still unread. I wondered if I could ring the hospital to find out how Jay was. Perhaps Sarah would ring me.

'I'm sure you are looking forward to it. Nice to know where you're going. It's all set out for you when you're young: school, university. Enjoy the last few years of it, won't you – you paint your own picture after that.'

'Can I get you anything, Andrea?' I said. 'Cup of tea, glass of something?'

'No, no – I'm fine.' She smiled patronisingly at my imitation of her cool, social manner. I did not know how to behave in front of her and she knew it. I did not want to talk about myself.

'God, yes,' she went on. 'You're lucky to have direction, Emily. Tom doesn't. I mean, he's had his year out and everything – fair enough – but suddenly one year stretches to two, and he's still at home. Sometimes I think it's understandable – he's so loved and spoilt here – but then I think *no*, where the hell's his am*bi*tion?'

I listened to the cars going by on the road outside.

'I mean there was that whole film school idea. God, I was excited when he wrote off. You have to play it cool as a mother, though. You certainly have to do that, or it gets dropped just to spite you. I'm no fool. I was just so *ha*ppy for him – you know, to have a *direction*.' She looked away and furrowed her brow, held her hands up –

'But somehow it disappeared. Nothing to do with me. It all just evaporated this summer and there's a pile of unopened brochures in the hall. Worse than ever. The ambition came – and now it's gone, like *that* –' she snapped her fingers. She liked to snap her fingers – she wanted you to appreciate she knew all about shocks. She smiled at me – gently.

'What's happened to Tom, Emily? What's happened to my son?' she said. Her face looked flushed.

'Nothing,' I told her.

'That's not what it looks like to me. What do you think – d'you think I don't notice? You think being twenty-five-odd years older makes me *blind* somehow? As if these things aren't within my range of understanding.' She shook her head. 'Jesus, you think you're all tragic heroes – *cos*mically misunderstood.'

'I don't think I'm anything at all, Andrea.'

'Don't you think I *know* what's been going on, Emily?'

I looked at the thin linen curtains, blue white where the sun caught them, soft grey in the shade.

'Don't you?'

'I don't know,' I told her. A sense that this might be it – that somehow she had found out about Simon and me – was almost luxurious, like a fever. I thought: any minute now I can lie down, give up.

She made an odd gesture, wiping her hand across her mouth.

'I can see what it is – of course I can. It's not as if I haven't had opportunities in my life to understand these things. I see the appeal – little girl by the roadside – *save* me! *save* me! The blonde hair, the big, grey eyes. I *get* it.'

'Are you talking about me?' I said.

She laughed bitterly, took her sunglasses off and shook her hair out. She laid the glasses in her lap – as if she might throw a punch and break them.

'Please don't play that with me. It doesn't work on women.'

'I'm not playing anything.' My voice sounded lifeless, as though I didn't know the language properly.

'My son is in love with you, Emily. You know *that*, do you?'

'Yes. That's what he says.'

She jumped up. It had been too much for her in the end to hear it stated.

'That's what he says,' she repeated. She walked over to the window and moved the linen curtain – looking out at nothing.

'I'm sorry, Andrea. I know he's unhappy. But you must know I didn't mean—'

'No, I'm sure you didn't.'

'Look, I'm going to leave him alone. I'm going to just disappear so he'll – he'll get over it.'

'D'you know what kind of a state he's in?'

'No.'

'Well, I wouldn't either if I couldn't read the signs. It's not like he'll *talk* to me.' She waved her hand in front of her face the way Tony had when he talked about all their houses, all the fuss, all the builders. 'Luckily, I've become an expert at reading *signs* over the years. An *ex*pert.'

She let the curtain drop and went on:

'The thing is, you look at Tom and you see someone with all the advantages in the world – young, ex*treme*ly good looking, all the clothes, the car. Well, not the car any more. But still, it looks great. It even convinces *me* sometimes. But when I really think about it, I think he's had a hard life, Emily. What do you grow up believing in if you have a father who... a mother smashed to pieces again and again? They're your forces of gravity, your parents, your sun and moon – misaligned.'

The mixture of sentimentality and bitterness made her speech lurid and it repulsed me. I wanted to get away from her, to just get out of the room.

'And children know, Emily – they *know*. Tom knew what his father was up to, I know he did. He felt for me all the way through it. He felt it as though he was *me*.'

I looked down. Yes, I bet you made sure he did, I thought. Her unhappiness was tyrannical. It would be the last thing standing.

She sighed.

'God – what his father was *"up to"* – makes it sound mischievous. When I think how Tom used to say things – *"I'll* look after you, Mummy", putting his arms round me – it breaks your heart. That boy is so vulnerable. Do you understand how vulnerable he is?'

I remembered her saying that to me at her garden party. The mother's warning – I had barely picked up on it. I did not want to look at her. She said too much. More than was decent. Was that it? I didn't care. I felt my voice gather strength.

'Andrea, that's not my fault,' I said.

She laughed hard.

'Beautiful. So like your mother.'

'*What*?'

'What I mean is, you *led him on*. I saw you – looking darling in your white dress, intimate chats on the kitchen doorstep. If you didn't want him, what the hell were you hanging around him so much for?'

Because I was lonely, I thought. The thing is, I am so lonely I can hardly breathe.

But I knew I had been wrong. I had been as unfair to him as you can be to another person. And he was vulnerable. She was right. I looked down at my hands.

'I didn't mean it. I didn't mean anything. I've never *meant* anything.'

Her face looked crazed and I couldn't watch it any more. I watched her skirt walking back across the room. I saw her legs bending, her hand reaching for her bag.

'You think I'm blind, Emily, right? Well if I am then maybe it's because I've walked bang, smack into one horrible truth again and again in this life. Maybe *finally* it's knocked me out. You want to know what it is – that truth? Because it'll even find you one day. It's that when you give your heart to someone and they decide they don't want it, you never really get it back.'

She looked at me – her eyes red and her lips pale and twitching. Then she walked out of the room.

I sat for a while, thinking. I thought about my Uncle Peter, Dad's brother. I go back to this memory a lot – a picnic we went on with Mum once, while Dad was working. My perfect, childhood day. We were all children that day – Mum and Peter too. Peter made up stories for us: there was a wind blowing in the long grass – it was a crashing sea, he said. A golden, magic sea. We rowed with the salad spoons. Peter put his tie round his head – I remember my mother laughing and laughing. We sang seafaring songs on the way home, all of us together. I thought: it could always be like this. Why isn't life always like this?

I remember Mum kissing Peter goodbye in the hallway that night.

'Oh Peter – be *ha*ppy,' she said. She put her hand on his cheek. 'Will you try?'

I was on the landing, unnoticed behind the banisters. I sank back, sensing their privacy.

'And you?' he said.

'Me? I am happy. I *am*.'

He kissed her cheek – and even then I knew the loud smacking sound of that kiss was full of grown-up anger with the world. I thought about our picnic and how we had all said we would do it again. But I knew the weather was not always that good for picnics. I looked at Dad's study door and felt a great wave of things I didn't understand fold over me – it was what crushed me against the wall when I sat in Irena's hallway. Was it strong enough to sweep away laughter, songs in the car? I knew wonderful things happened once and no one could promise they'd ever happen like that again. Suddenly I had a child's idea of how a person could get to look as sad as Uncle Peter.

Now I wonder if maybe I knew too early on that nothing lasted. Not childhood. Not love. Not marriage. The game I had played with my friend Nina at about that age – where she was the Daddy and I was the Mummy – was not about being grown-ups, it was about promises, about permanence. Her father sent her postcards from his new family home in America – she showed me: Mickey Mouse, Hollywood, Daffy Duck.

'We are man and wife, united in holy matrimony,' she used to say – in a Texan priest's voice she had heard on TV. She knew nothing lasted too.

And when we were too old for the game and one night I slept with her brother and she slept with his friend, she said, 'We're really married now' – and she giggled. We were sitting in the garage, frightened by our new experience, sharing a cigarette. I remember the sore, exciting feeling inside me, and thinking experience had literally stretched me. I can see how the smoke puffed out of her nose when she giggled. And I remember how we never really wanted to see each other again after that. The promises game had been rubbish for kids all along – and now she had said it outright: 'We're really married now', it was a silly joke. I walked home, shaking her off along with the dirty feel of her brother's body, the look of his screwed-up face.

Simon was nothing like that boy, that experience. What I loved about Simon was his faith in the world. What I loved about Simon was, he believed in love lasting. He needed to believe in love lasting as much as I did. He could hardly look at the empty place on Andrea's hand where her ring had been all those years. I heard his voice gently shrugging away chaos, making peace that first time at my parents' supper table. He had been as bad as the rest of us until Rachel got ill. Then he knew what it meant to love someone: Rachel was ill and he just sat by her bed. He had said so then. He had explained it all so beautifully for me.

I felt my hands shaking. It was a good joke, really – beautiful in its way. Elliptical – I loved someone for the way he said he loved someone else. My love negated itself. And did his love for me do the same? 'It's the way you seem to feel so hard for everyone else . . . It lights you up,' he had told me. So flattering. I only felt hard for myself now.

I felt the sweat on my head and in the folds of my eyelids. I ran upstairs to the bathroom and turned the shower on full, cold. I pulled my clothes off and stood under it, feeling it soak through my hair and pour in streams off my elbows. I held my face right under it, hearing it thundering on my eyes and nose, deafening and icy cold. It was like heavy rain.

There had been no rain for a long time. While I put my clothes back on I looked out at the garden, at the yellowish grass, the singed leaves. The man next door was using a watering can on his flowerbed. His dog was panting in a patch of shade behind him. The sky was the same rich blue it had been yesterday and the day before. Even with the cold water in my hair, I could already feel the heat swelling through me again.

I took Ellie's shoes from behind the bathroom door and ran down the stairs and out of the door. Andrea's car had gone. I crossed the road to her house. The small shoes were difficult to walk in, but I was already living out the sensations a few seconds ahead of me – the wooden door against my hand, the wet paint smell of the hallway.

I tried to move the cardboard box which was blocking the doorway – it was heavy and I had to kick it out of the way. I went in. I could hear a radio playing somewhere –

'This is the news at six o'clock . . .'

'Simon?' I called out. I heard a bang – possibly a stepladder being folded – and then his footsteps came quickly over the floorboards above me. He leant down from the top of the stairs, an expression of blank surprise on his face.

'What – what's happened? Is everything . . .' He was holding a tape measure. It flapped along the banisters slowly as he moved down. He looked like a sleepwalker. I stared at him hard, standing there halfway down the stairs, where his fear had stopped him.

'Emily?' His mouth sounded dry. 'Has something happened to you?'

'No,' I said. 'Nothing.'

And nothing had happened – to me and Simon, anyway. But everything had changed. Is the human imagination always so crass, so naive – always expecting the blinding event, when big changes in life are just a click in the brain?

He waited.

'You're scaring me. What's happened?' I started to cry and now he came down the stairs, glad to know what to do – there was a girl who was crying. He put his arm around me, took me into the kitchen.

'Emily, sit down,' he said. He pulled a box over for me and crouched beside it, holding my hand.

I think the way I cried then is a way you cry only once in your life. After that, it is just a kind of quotation from that first time; a phrase repeated, gradually losing its meaning, cloaking itself in secret purpose, bitterness. I had put love first – my love – and made a new gentle sense of the world. Now everything was ruined. And love ought to have brought the sky down with it – but it fell so eerily, without a sound. The tears soaked my face and neck.

'*Please,* Emily,' he said, after a while.

I looked at him. There was a streak of blue paint on his cheek. His eyes were narrowed, frightened looking. I felt sorry for him but the anger in me was stronger.

'We're liars,' I said.

'What?'

'There's no truth in any of this.'

'There is. What d'you mean? I don't lie to you.' He tightened his grip on my hand, lifted the linked fingers in front of my face. '*This* is not a lie.'

'It is, Simon.' I felt totally exposed – a child who has just realised she isn't invisible when she covers her own eyes.

'No, it isn't. Please, Emily, *please*. It isn't. I love you.' He had not actually said this to me before – I knew the guilt had stopped his mouth up. Now the words were out. And what an incredible effect they had. I felt as if violent weather – cold wind and rain – had been destroying the room, slapping the curtains up the walls, scattering papers – and now someone had quietly shut the window.

'Emily. Emily, I love you. It's OK,' he said. 'Come here –' and he kissed my mouth. We kissed each other softly for a long time.

When I think about it now, I wonder what Tom must have seen first. He came in through the garden, through the french windows into the kitchen. I wonder how the picture came into focus. I imagine him walking over the grass. I imagine it from his perspective, the soft thud of his shoes, our shapes bobbing up and down in the window frame in time to his footsteps. Did we become intelligible gradually, a little more with each step? And when he could see, did he take in the whole picture at once – Emily and Simon? Or did he just see a man and a girl – two strangers – kissing, out of context?

And when did he feel the wrong? Immediately, instinctively – as if he had seen a baby with a huge tumour, a plane falling out of the sky? Or more slowly, like a nightmare re-piecing in the conscious mind.

He was carrying something – an envelope of money and a box of picture hooks. He put the things down on the sideboard and said, 'Money for paint' – which is when we noticed him.

He looked at us quietly. He looked at us without any sign of surprise or emotion. I will never forget that quietness, the sweat on Simon's hand, the force field which shocked my mouth shut when I tried to speak. And Tom's words – 'Money for paint' – hanging, slipped into a pocket of electric significance, transformed into brutal poetry.

And then Tom walked away down the hall and we heard him kick the heavy box out of the doorway and then the front gate creaked as he opened it.

For a moment we didn't speak. Then Simon shook his head.

'It doesn't matter,' he said. 'He hates me. You can't hate a person more than Tom hates me.'

I felt sick. For a moment I thought I would be sick.

'But he'll tell Rachel,' I said. He looked at me.

'I mean it: it doesn't matter – it just doesn't matter.' He stood up; his eyes were shining and his face looked flushed as if we had just made love. 'Because *I'll* tell Rachel. I'll tell her. So it doesn't matter.' He laughed – it was such a strange, unnatural sound – and he stroked my hair. I tried to say something but the words were not right. Simon held my hand.

'Just because something starts the wrong way doesn't mean you can't make it better, does it? It's not cursed. I'm married – yes – but I'm young. I've made a mistake. People get married out of fear, pity, dependence. Maybe I did all of that. God, she was ill and I – I asked her and then it was too late. It gets too late so fucking easily.'

He walked over to the things Tom had left on the sideboard and picked them up, as if they were supercharged with the moment and he believed just touching them would push him further –

'I won't be manipulated. The heart fights back – it won't rest. It's why I don't sleep. Promises matter, but happiness matters more. Jesus, I tried to break it off and she just – she stopped eating, stopped drinking. She shut down. What could

I do? I thought: that must be love. I thought: no one will ever love me that much again and who the fuck am I to refuse it? I think I just wanted something pure, unquestionable. There is so much divorce in my family, Emily. So much *question*.'

I remembered him saying that to me before: 'How did you get yourself mixed up in our family, anyway? Our faithless bloody family,' he had said. He is no better than I am, I thought, and no worse for wishing things different.

He walked across the kitchen to me, smiling sadly, shaking his head again.

'Look I made a mistake. I'm young. The world won't collapse, will it? Wouldn't it be more wrong to stay with her now?'

'I don't know. I don't know what's wrong – what's *more* wrong. How are you supposed to know?'

'I'm so sorry, Emily – I made a mistake.'

'Don't. Please don't say sorry to me. It's her you should . . .' Was this the first time I had really thought about what she might feel? You think you are touching reality, but there is always more of it – brighter, sharper – just behind.

'I know, Em. I know. I've done everything wrong. But I love you.'

And the window shut softly on all the wind and rain again. I let him pull me up and put his arms around me. He said he would go to Edinburgh that night and see her in person. He would explain, he said. He would tell his wife he had made a mistake.

Chapter nine

We said goodbye on the doorstep. The gate banged into the fence and we both turned, startled and then laughed at ourselves. I think the world felt live with electricity to us both just then. Simon looked down and his face became serious

'So, I'll get the train up to Edinburgh tonight. I think it's best I do this straight away.'

'Yes,' I said. I was so happy I did not even want to meet the seriousness in Simon's face. I did not want to speak, to hear or see anything that wasn't my happiness. This is life, this is really life, I was thinking. Life was not unspoken resentments, secrets, making do with what had been spoilt – life felt like this, like hope.

'Em, look at me,' he said. '*Please* look at me. This is going to take a while, OK? I'll call as soon as I can – but you'll have to give it a day or two.'

'Of course, look, I understand. Don't worry.'

'Em, don't *you* worry. This is all going to be all right.'

'Yes it is,' I said. Then I kissed him and he walked off towards the tube station leaving me on the doorstep with that sun burning on my face.

I thought it would be impossible to sleep that night. Apart from the fact that my body was used to sleeping in the day, I had never felt so excited. My thoughts went round an obstacle course, swerving between dreams about the future and whatever my imagination pushed in their way. I saw myself and Simon living together while I did my degree. Couples could get flats together from universities – I knew that. Couples. I thought maybe he would start his teacher training course now. All of my unread books, his unmade plans – for a moment I wondered if he had been as unhappy as I was. Perhaps we had both just needed to be happy before we could get started.

And we would be happy. We would have a big desk and do our work opposite each other with a window and a lovely garden view in between. We would have a wooden bed, and a little kitchen with the sun always on the table and the smell of toast and jam and coffee. Maybe we would keep his old red car – or perhaps we would need the money and get bicycles instead. We could ride off for picnics by the river. I could see our bicycles lying against each other in the grass. There would be a haze of mayflies. Us laughing a little way off.

When I did fall asleep there were no dreams. I slept deeply

and woke up at around ten the next day. And as soon as my eyes opened, I sat up and smiled. What other reaction was there to that new world? I took a long bath and washed my hair and put on a clean white shirt and shorts. Then I combed my hair in the sun until it was dry and shone whitish gold. It made me smile to see myself looking better in the hall mirror. There were croissants in the kitchen and I heated one up and took it out into the garden with my coffee. Dad was out there walking up and down, which is what he does when he finds his work difficult.

'Morning, Dad,' I said. I was blinking in the sunlight.

'*Morning*? Middle of the night for you, isn't it?'

I smiled at him.

'I'm a reformed character,' I said. 'I'm going to make use of my days. No more moping. No more lying in. Carpe diem.'

'What on earth has brought this on? I will tell you one story, Emily. I had a friend who was a terrible alcoholic and a heavy smoker. Enormous fun. Old Jakey. Drank his whole inheritance. Anyway, one day he had the misfortune to find God *and* a Harley Street specialist. Gave up the fags and the booze at once. And d'you know what happened?' He dislodged a stone in the flowerbed with his shoe. 'He went into a coma.'

I laughed.

'What exactly is the moral of that story, Dad?'

'Oh – don't try to do too much at once, I suppose. Try giving up moping, say, *or* lying in bed all day.'

'Or I might go into a coma?'

'Metaphorically speaking. Look at your mother's friends from the church.'

'Oh, Dad.'

'Voltaire has a good formula. He says don't let the best be the enemy of the good. Idealism does a lot of damage, you know. And it always fails.'

I held the croissant out to him.

'Want a bite?'

'Thanks.' He bit it out of my hand and we both laughed. He handed it back and sat down on the grass beside me for a moment.

'You know Em, it does mystify me . . .'

'What?

'Well, you're quite a pretty girl but you do seem to dress like a Boy Scout.'

I looked down at my khaki shorts and laughed.

'Don't girls wear skirts any more? Pretty dresses?'

'Yes they do,' I said. 'Don't you look at girls any more?'

Immediately I wished I hadn't said it, but he smiled and sighed. 'Oh, I suppose I do, Em. I just can't remember why.'

We sat silently for a moment and I thought how lovely it was to be talking happily with him. I looked at his worn old corduroy trousers, the shirt with the faded ink stain by the pocket. He is still good looking, I thought. I could see why Mum – Irena – would have found him attractive. Then he tapped his polished shoes together and stood up.

'Thank you,' he said.

'What for?'

'I don't know what you did, but you've had a magical effect on me. While we were talking I formulated my whole argument – Venetian economic policy in the fourteenth century.' He ruffled my hair. 'We must chat like this more often.' And then he rushed back into the house ten years younger than when I found him.

I smiled and shook my head, because nothing could have hurt me that morning. I finished the coffee and the warm croissant. Then I smoked a cigarette and thought about my clothes. It was true – I did dress like a boy. Even Ellie's clothes were sexier than mine. I thought about Sarah and all her miniskirts, her high heels. My friends had always teased me for going out in jeans and trainers. I thought about Rachel – her black floral shift dress cut to cling to her waist, to fall low beneath that sharp collarbone of hers.

I looked like a child. My one dress was white and shapeless and Mum had bought it for me when I was fourteen. I needed clothes that were more like me. I needed something to wear to meet Simon. A happiness dress, I thought – I had made myself smile again.

But of course I had no money. I had spent all my babysitting earnings long ago, and under the pretence of needing to study my books for university, I had not applied for the waitressing job I should have got. Tom had paid for everything when we went out. I looked down at the old shorts and felt a pang of anger – why couldn't my parents be more generous? It was OK if it was for books, but there was no point in asking for money for anything else – it had to be earned. I had heard Mum and Ellie just the day before.

'You'll have to get a Saturday job, then.'

'But why? You've got plenty of money. It's only £50, Mum.'

'Firstly we haven't got plenty of money, because it costs us all we've got to live here and send you to a good school and so on. But secondly Ellie, Dad and I always agreed you should save your own money up for things that weren't strictly necessary.'

I went into the kitchen and put my cup in the dishwasher, then I brushed my hands off on my shorts. I walked over to the mantelpiece and took the lid off the pot where Mum puts the housekeeping money and the money for the cleaning lady. She would be doing the big supermarket shop tomorrow and she always got money out in advance. There was £150 in there. I looked at it in my hand for a moment – two fifties, two twenties and a ten – and then I put it back into the box and pushed the lid down carefully.

Then I opened it again and stuffed the money in my pocket and ran upstairs and out of the door.

I kept walking away from the house. My fingers felt the notes in my pocket. I felt elated – like the child who sends a stone hard at the glinting window. I ran all the way to the tube station.

I got a train to Knightsbridge, where Sarah bought most of her clothes. I had walked past all the sparkling windows there on one of my night walks before Simon. I had even seen a dress I had thought was beautiful. I was not sure it would still be there, but if it was, I would buy it. It was strange to think I had looked at it – just a girl behind the glass – and now I would have a reason to wear it.

I walked down Knightsbridge through the crowds feeling a kind of blissful sorrow for everyone I passed. Poor them – I had taken the greatest happiness in the world, I had got there first. The feeling was so powerful as it rose up in me, past my lungs, making my breath faster, past my heart, that I had to close my eyes to contain it.

There was one dress left in my size. I lifted the hanger and spread the skirt out over my arm. It was made of two layers of fine red chiffon, printed very softly with a pattern of roses. The neck was low and studded with tiny dark red beads. It was £155 – the most expensive thing I would ever have owned. I felt my mouth go dry. I had seen Sarah spend that much before, and I had enjoyed choosing with her because she could look so pretty, but I had never seen myself in her place.

I had never really seen myself anywhere. But now there I was, in that dress, at the station, or at a little café – meeting Simon.

I had just enough with the money I had stolen and the change in my pocket. I did not try it on. My hands felt too shaky to undo my clothes. I put the dress on the counter by the till and pushed the bundle of crumpled notes and coins into the girl's hand.

'It's a gorgeous dress,' she said as she folded it. 'It's really romantic. It'll look amazing with your hair.' She smiled at me – and I thought yes, it will. It will look great on me.

'Is it for anything special?'

'It's for a wedding,' I said. She nodded and I wondered why I had said that. Lies were coming so easily. It's a beautiful lie, though, I thought – true in a sense. I walked out of the shop with the plastic bag in my hand, into the crowds again.

When I got home, I put the dress in my cupboard behind the rest of my clothes. No one would come into my room, but I wanted to hide it. The ruffled hem showed dark red behind the bottom of my winter jacket. It was almost impossible to imagine winter coming – the summer had been so long. The coat looked heavy and stifling. It reminded me of the past, and I thought: I will never ever wear that sad old thing again. All my clothes would need to be new now.

I went downstairs to get my books off the hall table where they had sat since I bought them. I made lunch for myself, and took some cushions and a rug out into the garden. I lay in the shade with my head propped on the cushions and ate the sandwiches and read all afternoon. Life is starting, I told myself again. For the first time, I pictured with real excitement the lecture halls I would be sitting in. I imagined writing essays late in the library, my pen going over the pages, books open all over a large table in front of me.

It was difficult to concentrate on the words I was reading. Sentences about the French Revolution ran imperceptibly into dinners with Simon, candles on saucers around the room. We were going to be so happy. A few times I lost track of my book altogether and had to jump up and walk quickly around the garden to calm down. There was a strong breeze and I listened to it flapping the clean laundry next door and then I lay down on the rug again and picked up my book.

It rained that evening and the water darkened the dry leaves and the grass. It spattered hard on the paving stones and brought out the smell of the bricks. I walked around the block a few times, past the café I had watched Rachel and Simon in. None of that mattered now – my hope buffeted the pain of all those old pictures away. The sky was lavender and the grass looked fresh by the little park. Three boys were smoking together on the climbing frame. The smoke trailed across the tarmac, past their bikes.

My mother made Spanish omelettes that night. The olive

oil and the onions smelt strong and delicious. I shook dressing over the tomatoes in the big white bowl. Dad came down when I called him and he opened a bottle of wine.

'Where's Ellie?' I said. Dad filled my glass.

'I'll try calling again,' Mum said. She walked over to the kitchen phone. 'I'm hoping Jessica's mother's dropping her back. She promised she'd be home for supper.'

I looked out of the window and watched the trees blow.

'No,' Mum said, 'still no answer. It's 8.30.' She hung up.

'Don't get in a panic, Jane. She'll come crashing in any second. Come on, let's eat. This looks delicious,' Dad said.

Mum looked at her watch. 'OK. They've probably stopped for milkshakes or something, haven't they? I get the impression Jessica gets what Jessica wants.'

'Jane, Richard will be here in about an hour to give me a lift up to this conference. Shall we eat?'

'You're going away?' I asked.

'It's just a one day-er, I'll be back tomorrow night. Come and sit down and have a glass of wine, Jane.'

Mum smiled and held a glass out to him and he poured it very full.

'Hey, don't get me drunk,' she said. She looked at me and we laughed.

'You've never been drunk, Mum.'

'Oh, I have.'

Dad covered his eyes and Mum laughed again.

'Just once. Gin. Someone gave me a glass of neat gin – and because I thought all drink was so disgusting, I just knocked it back. You know – sort of held my nose. Anyway I was very drunk in about half an hour – it was like being at the bottom of a swimming pool, I remember, with everyone watching around the edges. I just lay there on a big cushion.'

'Beached on a bean bag she was,' Dad said. 'I was trying to be terribly impressive to someone . . . Professor Saxby, I think it was . . . yes, I think it was him.'

'And then I was very sick and after that I was completely sober and everyone else at the party was getting drunk. It was incredibly boring, actually.'

We all laughed together and Dad said, oh well, cheers.

My happiness is making everything better, I thought. Mum clinked my glass and smiled at me. I remembered the beautiful dress in my cupboard.

Later that night, when I was in my room, I took the dress out and took off my shorts and shirt. I stood barefoot in front of my mirror and lowered it over my head. It felt weightless and expensive. I kept my eyes away from the mirror until I had zipped up the back and then I looked. I pulled the elastic band out of my hair and stood up straight. I smiled at my own reflection. The dress was a bit loose around the waist, but I loved it. My appearance surprised me. The dark red fabric made my skin and my hair shine very pale and my eyes looked blue against them. Maybe I am prettier than Rachel, I thought. I felt the hate well up in me.

And with the hate came fear. I sat on my bed and lit a cigarette, watching myself in the mirror. I watched the smoke curling out of my mouth. Simon had said to give it a day or two. They would have a lot to talk about. I didn't even want to imagine it. I wrung the thought out of my head and stared at my reflection instead. There is no place for guilt, I told myself. Even jealousy could go now. I was going to be happy. Simon was going to be happy.

Two people happy or three people unhappy – you choose, God, I thought.

But what did God have to do with it? I lit another cigarette and then, from who knows where, something Andrea had said the first time I met her came back to me: 'I sometimes think getting older is about every year of your life understanding another terrible thing people do.' And my mind seemed to follow her words with some purpose of its own, back to the day Irena's husband came and stood on our doorstep.

I must have been five years old. It was a cold day and the rain was coming down hard behind him. The cold air blasted over me when I opened the door.

'Is your father here? I need to speak with your father,' he said. He had a Russian accent, it went with the cold. I remember staring at his face. I had seen it in photographs along Irena's hall: Stefan catching a fish, Stefan with his arm round another man, holding a glass up at the camera, his face one big smile. I looked at him then and thought his face looked like a jigsaw puzzle coming to pieces. I must have been staring dumbly, looking frightened, because he sank down on to his haunches and smiled desperately at me.

'Will you go get Daddy for me?'

I could see the sweat on his forehead. He smelt terrible, his face looked scratchy with stubble and his eyes were red.

And then I remember suddenly snapping back into awareness: my mother was in the kitchen making supper. Perhaps she had dropped a pan at that moment. I was literally struck dumb with panic, seeing that urgent brightness in his face.

Maybe Stefan being here would be part of Dad's secret, I thought. Should I just slam the door? Would I be sent to bed for being rude? Was it all right to tell Mum or not?

Then I heard my father's voice coming from the kitchen – he and my mother were talking. I must have asked Stefan to wait on the doorstep. I think I remember him lighting a cigarette, turning and blowing on his hands to warm them.

I ran down the stairs to the kitchen and did the only thing I could think of. I rushed up to my mother, put my arms round her and kissed her. Then I did the same to Dad and whispered in his ear, 'Tomasz's Daddy's here' – we never said her name to each other. He stood up, saying he felt like doing the crossword and he was just popping out for a newspaper. Mum turned round from the fridge and looked out of the window. Water was running in streams over the glass.

'Goodness – in this weather? Don't float away, will you?' She smiled at him.

Please float away, I thought. I saw him racing away from us on a huge dirty wave – like the waves at Brighton with all the old bottles and plastic bags. I followed him silently upstairs and watched him go to the door, pulling on his coat.

'We can't talk here, Stefan,' he said. The door closed behind them.

Then I went back down to my mother and helped her wash the potatoes. I wanted to tell her Dad had just told her a lie. Mrs Faulkner said a lie was a sin and it made God sad. I looked at Mum smiling at me, saying we could keep some potatoes and cut them into shapes for prints, and I thought: Dad tells you lies and you are stupid, stupid, stupid because you never guess. I wanted to knock the pile of white plates beside me smashing on to the floor. I cut my finger on her knife and I didn't say. I put my finger in my mouth and I ran upstairs with the funny taste of blood.

I flicked the ash off my cigarette. Had my father been in love with Irena? Had he loved her the way I loved Simon?

'How did you get so innocent, Emily?' Dad had said to me a little while ago, teasing me. No, I thought, that cool, sarcastic mind had never loved anyone the way I loved Simon. I would never understand what he had done. If Andrea was right and you just had to get older to understand why people did things, then I knew I would never get that old. The same rules did not apply to me and Dad. As for what he thought of me – I was not innocent. I would never let myself be innocent, like Mum. I pushed the cigarette out so hard the ashtray spun on to the floor.

Now, looking back, I wonder if people ever know the difference in themselves or in others, between innocence and sophistication, sophistication and innocence. Perhaps you only ever know which was which when it is too late. Or maybe there is just not much difference. How much lying does innocence require, after all – from yourself, from others – to maintain itself? And how much innocence does it take to make you feel you are in control, knowing, sophisticated?

I looked at myself in my new grown-up red dress. Then I looked down at my mobile phone by my bed, willing it to ring. And when it finally did, it rang right in the middle of my head, my lungs.

It was Sarah.

'Hi, Em. Listen, d'you know where Tom is?' she said. 'Ronnie and I are just sitting here like lemons.' I heard the sound of a bar or a restaurant behind her. I listened to her swallow some of her drink – the ice, the fizz. Could they – could Tom – really be going out drinking while Jay was in hospital? Then Ronnie said something to her.

'Where? Oh yeah,' Sarah said back. 'Fuck, Em – sorry to bother you – we think that's him in a taxi now.' She said goodbye and I put the phone down. Had I actually spoken, I wondered. I let my head fall on the pillow and brought my knees up to my chest, feeling sick with fear.

I looked across at the mirror again. The red dress spilled out over the unmade bed. It stood out very dark against the sheets. I pictured my mother opening the box on the mantelpiece before she went shopping. She would put her hand in, frown, then she would lift it up and look inside it. I imagined her calling up the stairs to my father. The voice made my head ache. I stared at my face:

'Who have you done the most harm to?' I asked myself. 'Simon? Rachel? Tom? Or yourself?'

It felt suffocatingly hot in my room just then and I got up and pushed the window wide open. The sky was cool and clear and I took a deep breath. This is not about harming people, I told myself. If I had learnt anything from my parents, it was that being good, as my mother had, could be just as harmful to another person, as doing wrong. Maybe Dad could have been happier – kinder. Maybe we let people become monsters if we aren't brave enough to challenge them.

I felt angry and ridiculous. Questioning who I had done the most harm to was far too simplistic. Because this was about truth – the absolute truth. Not short-term pain. Simon and Rachel were unhappy together. Sure there were moments between them, I could imagine – like the kiss outside the café, the way they looked together under the tree in Andrea's garden. But underneath that Tom had told me Rachel was neurotic, always getting headaches, refusing to eat. 'Quite a hassle for Simon,' he said. I had seen the tension between them myself, at Andrea's house, when Rachel sent him for painkillers and suddenly he looked so weary. He took her lunch up a little later on a tray. That was Rachel.

Simon had said he had made a mistake when he married her. That was the truth, and strangely, it had taken lying to uncover it. How much harm would have been done if Simon had stayed married to Rachel, letting her become more neurotic, more tyrannical? There was a lesson for my simplistic mind in that. Then I thought about Tony and the way I had judged him when he took me and Tom out for dinner. What the hell had I known then?

After that I lay down again with the phone in my hand, and with what must have been an instinct for psychological survival, I fell asleep.

At around two there was a knock on my door. Simon, I thought. Simon. But, of course it could not have been him. My mother came in. She stood in the shaft of light from the doorway, still fully dressed. I checked the clock again: 2 a.m.

'Mum?'

'Em, I don't know what to do,' she said. I sat up.

'What's going on?'

'She hasn't come back. I called everyone I could think of and then I finally called Susan Martin and woke her up about ten minutes ago and she said Jessica's family are all on holiday in Spain.'

I stood up and switched the light on. Then I went over and put my arms round her.

'Mum, she's probably gone to a party and got a bit tipsy on cider or something. I bet you she'll come wobbling up the stairs any minute.'

'D'you think?' She walked over to the ashtray I had left broken on the floor and picked it up absentmindedly, dropping the cigarette butts in the bin. This is what she does – she clears up, I thought. I hate her. She could have been happy like me.

Then I thought about Ellie. She had never done anything like this before and I knew it. She was full of argument, but she never actually did anything. How typical of her to be found out, when I had got away with things all my life – sneaking out, coming home undiscovered. I got away with everything, Ellie got caught. Now I wonder who was more fortunate.

'Why would she tell a lie about Jessica? They're all in Spain, Em.'

'Oh Mum, let's go down to the kitchen and have a cup of tea. We'll listen out for her.' I rubbed her arm and then we walked down the stairs together. 'Bet you she's back in half an hour,' I said.

At six thirty she had still not come back. We sat with our cups in the sitting room, listening to the empty street. Mum was on the sofa opposite me with her face clenched up at the window. I watched her for a while.

'You really love us, don't you?' I said.

She looked at me sadly.

'I'm sorry,' I said. 'I know you love us.'

'Why do you question everything, Em? Let yourself believe in a few things.'

I laughed bitterly – Dad's laugh.

'Like God, you mean.'

She looked away from me and I felt anger building. I hated her quiet, long-suffering belief.

'God's done you so much good, after all,' I said.

'Emily, you can't begin to know that.'

Just shut up, I told myself. Leave her alone.

'Look, I just want to be happy,' I said. 'I don't see things the way you do. I couldn't live like you. Never.'

'Why are you so angry, Emily?'

'If you really want to know it's because I think you live in ignorance,' I said. 'It's wilful.'

She closed her eyes for a moment. Then she said, 'Things are more complicated than you know.'

'Oh, I know it all. Every bit of it,' I said.

'You know the facts, Emily. I know you know the facts – your dad, that woman. I know you know all about that part.'

I looked down at my lap – I was still wearing the red dress. In her panic she seemed not to have noticed. I pulled the skirt down towards my knees.

'When did he tell you about her?' I asked.

'I knew anyway – after a while. Of course I did. There were dinner parties we all went to. They were pretty unsubtle about it.'

I closed my eyes – I could imagine.

'And you did nothing. You just gave up?'

'No. I went on living. I never gave up – *he* did.'

We sat silently for a moment and then she said, 'He won't

forgive himself, Emily. You can't love or be loved if you hate yourself that much. Anyway, it's too late for that now – we're like brother and sister now. And I know that may sound terrible to you at your age, but it's not. It's more than you think.'

'I don't understand. Aren't you lonely? Don't you want love – real love?'

'Real love? It is real love. What you're talking about – lust, insecurity – it passes. Maybe I've never believed in that kind of love anyway.'

'It's there,' I said. 'It exists.'

'Does it? Doesn't it always come with pain – end in disappointment? The more I've lived, the simpler everything's seemed. If I had to define it I'd say love is trying never to cause people pain.'

'That's giving up,' I said. 'That's just cowardice dressed up to look noble.'

She looked out of the back window, into the garden. I do not notice it often, but my mother has a beautiful face. She pays no attention to her looks – they are there almost in spite of her. A bit of an embarrassment to her asceticism. She tucked her grey hair behind her ears.

'You remember Dad and I went to stay with that friend of his – Jean-Luc – in France a few years ago? Well, they were busy talking about work and academic things I don't really know about, so I said to Dad I was going to go off for a few days. And I did – I went up to a little monastery in the hills I'd heard about. Where they do Catholic retreats.'

I imagined with discomfort the way Dad would have teased her about this. I tugged the skirt down again.

'Anyway, while I was there I did a lot of thinking – about

our family. About how to make it happier. In the end I thought I needed some advice. There was only one monk there who could speak good enough English. He was a man about my age now, very quiet and peaceful looking. And I told him the lot – about Dad and that woman, the poor husband calling me night after night. I told him about you and Ellie – how Dad treated you both so differently.'

'He's been cruel to Ellie,' I said.

'I don't think he's been great to you, Em. You see through him.' She looked right at me and I thought the tenderness in her face would make me cry, so I dug my nails into my hands.

'Anyway,' she said, 'I sat in that beautiful, simple monastery and told the whole complicated story. I must have talked for over an hour. And you know what he said – at the end of it all?'

She smiled and looked at me. There were tears in her eyes.

'He said, "I'm so sorry. I don't know what to say – you see, I just make the cheese."'

'But that's terrible,' I said.

'I just make the cheese,' she repeated, smiling. 'And I thought: yes, so do I.'

I looked at her, disbelieving, again hating the complacency I saw in her.

'And everything falls apart,' I said, 'when you could do so much more.'

'What has fallen apart, Emily? We're all here, in this house. I'm here – loving you, loving Dad.'

'You still love him?'

'Of course I do. I used to think I should never have got married – that it wasn't fair on your dad, because his nature was so much more passionate, more complicated than mine. More sexual, I suppose. I thought I'd starved him – that Irena was all my fault.'

'Oh, Mum.' I remembered her turning away from the sink, smiling, younger, my child's arms round her neck. And I remember that kiss. Then I ran over to Dad and did the same. That whisper: 'Tomasz's Daddy's here.' A kiss, a whisper. The laugh between me and Simon the first time we met – Tom looking over. What tiny events define us and move us into the future.

'But I did marry him, Em,' Mum said, 'and he married me. I offered him a divorce, when it all happened – and he didn't want one. Because he needs me – someone to make the cheese. He couldn't live without me. And for all his sarcasm, I couldn't live without him. Marriage runs very deep, Emily.'

Her gentle words seemed to knock the life out of me. I did not ask her anything else. We sat looking out of the window and waiting and every so often I would look across at my mother and think how little I knew about her life. I had assumed so much, judged her every gesture and reaction by my own standards – and missed the point of her. I hated her and loved her more than I ever had, for that ethereal absence of hers. Good luck to you, I thought. I hope you are peaceful at heart. And I hope you are lonely, lonely, lonely.

The world felt empty and echoing as it had all my life. Nobody watching, no one to say what was right or wrong. I had told myself that feeling had gone for ever, but really it had been there even with Simon, when he slept beside me on that dusty mattress, between those bare walls. The world was like that room – things moved in, moved out and it was empty again, the happy couple gone – who knew why?

A short while later, there was the sound of a car stopping a little way down the road. A door slammed and then the car reversed away again. My mother and I looked at each other. A few moments later Ellie's key was scraping around the lock. My mother ran out into the hall and opened the door, upsetting Ellie's balance. She fell forward into Mum's legs.

'Where have you been? Where have you been, Ellie?'

Ellie had started to cry.

'Mum,' she said. Her voice sounded thick and slurring. She sat back on the floor, her head thudding against the radiator. Mum looked round desperately at me.

'She's just drunk, Mum,' I said. I went forward and took one of Ellie's arms. 'We'll have to carry her up to bed.'

'Wanna go to bed,' Ellie sighed. 'Up to bed.'

'Oh my God,' Mum said, 'I've never seen anyone this drunk.'

We carried her up together, straining under the dead weight, knocking a vase off the shelf along the stairs. It bounced down the stairs and smashed against the banisters. Mum caught my eye as it broke.

I could smell dope and alcohol on Ellie's clothes and when her eyes rolled towards mine for a moment, they were bloodshot and the pupils were dilated. Maybe she had taken coke or ecstasy, I thought. I said nothing to Mum. She did not seem ill – just wasted.

We took her clothes off and put her old Daffy Duck T-shirt on her and tucked her in. Mum got her a glass of water and put a bowl by her bed. When she turned the light off, Ellie cried out, 'No, please. Please . . . *Em.*'

'I'll sit with her for a bit,' I said. Mum nodded. She looked old suddenly after a night without sleep. 'Don't worry, Mum. She'll sleep it off,' I told her.

Mum walked towards the doorway and then she turned around. She looked at Ellie and then at me. 'I want you to know I listened to everything you said earlier, Em. I just want you to know that,' she said. The words were heavy with emotion. Her voice always gives her away – it is as sensitive to her feelings as a musical instrument. How could I begin to believe she was happy as she was? Just leave me out of it, I thought – out of your apathy and your emotion. I just want to go deaf. She looked away.

'Is that what you bought with the money, Em – that dress you're wearing?'

'Yes,' I said. She nodded again and closed the door behind her.

I waited for Ellie to fall asleep, thinking about all the times I had sat outside her door doing just the same when she was a little girl. A deep sense of dread built up in me about where she had been that night, because for all their big talk, their hair dye and bright lipstick, her friends were just children. I could not imagine them all buying drugs together. They would be too scared. I could not think how Ellie had got herself into that state.

I looked at her, at the eye make-up caked and smeared around her eyes, the wine stains around her mouth. I started to cry – and I suppose I was crying for myself. I want my innocence back, I thought, please give it back to me, someone.

Chapter ten

Our instinct for survival is ingenious, and it will work against us like all our good qualities. We can use it to deceive ourselves. I waited for Simon to call and there was nothing all that day. But it didn't matter. Just as his habit of leaving the door open for me was enough to destroy all my fear and jealousy before we met, he had told me he loved me and thrown a golden net over our future together.

Friends rang my mobile occasionally, unaware of the blow it gave me to read the wrong name on the little screen. I left all their calls unanswered; only wanting to listen to messages. Ronnie had called and left a message saying the operation on Jay's neck had gone well. I felt great relief for his mother – but only for a few seconds.

It seemed almost dangerous to think about anyone else –

my whole life was balanced on that single point in time where my hand touched the ringing phone and all the waiting was over. Maybe I thought I only needed to concentrate hard enough to bring it about. I suppose that is the illusion we all have about the importance of our own minds. It takes so much disappointment to make us realise how powerless we are against the force of another person's life – we need to feel it thunder past us, oblivious, like an express train.

Ellie slept until around three and came out of her room looking pale and sick. I asked her if she was all right and she nodded and pulled the bathroom door shut hard behind her. Fine, I thought, you deal with your stupid hangover on your own. Mum told me later that Ellie had come down rather formally to her room and promised never to do it again. There was nothing said about my dress. Within that vacuum of waiting for Simon to call, it seemed right that my actions should have had no consequences.

That evening Dad came back and Mum gave him a toned-down version of what Ellie had done.

'Oh well, I'm sure the hangover's been punishment enough,' he said. He looked at her over the table, staring down at her plate. 'Hasn't it, Eloise?'

'Yes,' she said. She still looked very pale and you could see she did not want to eat anything.

Later, when Mum took away Ellie's untouched plate, Dad said, 'Oh dear oh dear,' and shook his head. He was laughing – he seemed almost proud of her, as if he enjoyed the thought of her liking drink just the way her father did.

'Mum, can I go?' Ellie said.

'Yes, darling – you go to bed early. It's probably the best thing for you.' Mum got up to kiss her good night, which is not something she normally does. It looked forced. Ellie ran up the stairs as if she hadn't noticed.

'D'you think she's all right?' I said.

'Ashamed of herself,' Dad said. He brushed crumbs off his shirt and looked up brightly. '*Thoroughly* ashamed of herself, I should think.'

I could only imagine his strange elation was a kind of relief – that he wasn't the only one in trouble with Mum for drinking. He is like a child, I thought. And then I remembered thinking the same thing of Mum a little while ago when she pretended to Dad that all the wine was finished. Suddenly his 'drinking problem' seemed like a strange little game between them. I felt resentful that my emotions had been drawn into it. Their relationship was unintelligible to me – a dark space sparking with contradictions and an arid kind of satisfaction I had never noticed before. Maybe they deserve each other, I thought.

I watched Dad folding the napkins into the napkin rings. This is his one job around the house, because he likes doing it.

'Shall we have coffee in the garden, John?' Mum said. He smiled his half-smile.

'Mmm. Why not?'

She looked at me.

'Oh, I won't thanks, Mum – I've got to get on with my reading list.'

And I went upstairs and waited for Simon to call.

I wanted to pray that he would call soon, but I thought if there is a God, he will not be on my side. He will be on Mum's side – or that stupid monk who made the cheese, or Mrs Faulkner with the crooked eye. Maybe I should pray to the devil, I thought.

The argument did not last long. There is just nobody and the sky, I told myself, and you know it. But maybe that phone will ring.

Two days later there had still been no call. I felt I had exhausted every possible explanation in my mind. I had imagined Rachel hysterical, threatening to harm herself, Simon completely taken in. (I didn't allow myself to think her pain would be genuine.) I had imagined some terrible misjudged surprise – that he had called to say he was coming and she had made a special dinner for him, invited people she was working with. Perhaps he just hadn't been able to say it right away.

And if he hadn't said it, would he have made love to her again that night? That I couldn't believe – my nails drew blood from the palms of my hands I did not believe it so much.

I lay out in the garden with a book on my chest and closed my eyes against the sun. I watched the colours dancing under my eyelids. Once, when my eyes opened, I saw Ellie at the bathroom window. I waved and smiled at her, but she seemed not to notice me. She still seemed ill or upset about something – no loud music, no giggling phone calls or arguments with Mum – and I knew I ought to check she was all right. But the idea of listening to the details of another person's life made my eyes close and my head sink back, feeling dizzy, on to the grass.

In the evenings I read in my room or looked out of the window for Simon's car. He had said there was a lot to talk through with Rachel. Of course there was, even I understood that. Even a child like me who stole money for a grown-up dress could understand that. Give it a couple of days, he told me. The phrase reminded me of something Tony said to Simon when he came to take me and Tom out to dinner. Andrea had just walked away hurt by seeing her ex-husband again. Tony sighed.

'Don't worry, Simon, it's a bit soon, that's all. There's a rhythm to everything.' What dirty lessons we pass on to each other, I thought. How to betray politely. Now I was relying on wisdom like that.

By that evening it had been three days. Even the thought that he would leave me waiting that long felt like a kind of treachery. The truth was I could not imagine what had happened. I had decided early that morning that I would have to accept that something had gone wrong.

Something – but what? I wished Simon and I had stayed as we were, never been found out and forced to this remote point. I missed even those pathetic certainties of our times together, the supper in his bag, the mattress in the hall, that sense of containment between those empty walls. I think all I have ever wanted is that sense of containment, however temporary it turned out to be.

But something had gone wrong – something unnamed and belonging to a world I had no control over. The world the Lebanese couple had disappeared into. Maybe that realisation will always be in my memory, just as it came, in the blue-grey morning, with the sad music of that rubbish truck trailing away down the road.

At around nine that night, I heard the bathroom door opening and the sound of the bath draining. I went out and Ellie was walking towards her room wrapped up in her big pink towel. Her hair was wet and uncombed, her eyes were red, like a child who has been swimming.

'All right?' I said. 'Want a cigarette or anything? I've got lots.'

'No thanks.'

I put on an expression of horror and pretended I was feeling her forehead for a fever. The skin was very dry under my fingers. It was an awkward joke. Her eyes met mine and then she pulled away from me.

'I'm just going to go to bed,' she told me. She shut the door behind her. I went and stood outside it for a moment and listened to her moving her things around. I felt very lonely and wanted to talk to her.

But what could I say to her and what could she possibly say in response? I thought about simplifying the story for her, saying I had been dropped by a new boyfriend and felt terrible about it – that way it would sound like the things she and her friends talked about on the phone. And it would be so lovely, I thought, to have a bit of sympathy – even if it was for something that had not really happened to me. But I could not bring myself to tell any more lies and the real facts of the situation would be too complicated for her to understand. Or too humiliating for me to tell her. I have always enjoyed being looked up to by her – I know I have. I need her reliance on me desperately.

We all know where we stand, really, I think. I am better looking than her, more intelligent – who knows why? Who's to say it will make me happier? People just can't bear to admit these things to each other, and so they bind us invisibly, through guilt and pity, admiration and jealousy. Again I find myself asking whether it is ever worth knowing the reasons behind love.

Late that night, I heard the bathroom door click shut again. I put my book down and called out to her, 'You OK, Ellie?'

But she hadn't heard me over the running bath water. With that tiny part of my mind which was not concerned with myself it occurred to me that this was the third bath she had taken that day. I went out into the hall again and listened outside the door. I thought I could hear her crying. I glanced at her bedroom door. It was shut and I could see underneath that the lights were off. I called out to her again:

'Ellie? Is everything all right?'

There was a pause, the sound of something dropped into the water.

'Just having a quick bath.'

'OK.'

I could not think why she seemed so anxious and quiet. Mum had accepted her apology about staying out and she was not in any trouble. I listened again and this time I was sure I could hear her crying. The sound made me angry – she had no idea what sadness felt like, I thought. I would give anything to have her stupid problems. I pushed open her bedroom door with a harsh curiosity – as if, after all, her life might be a light distraction for a bit.

I had never seen her room look like that. Ellie is a collector; she has always treasured things while I have always lost them. I often think of her room as it was when she was a child, all her toys arranged in rows, her marbles, her lock boxes of precious letters and drawings. '*Please* look after it,' she says to me sternly if I borrow something from her – she knows that difference between us as well as I do.

The lights were off and the curtains were still open. The room was stuffy with the smell of sleep. I could feel the disorder around me, even in the dark. I switched on the lamp. There were wet towels all around the floor, clothes, old photos of her friends from junior school. Friends who didn't come round any more. The drift of people away from us.

All summer there had been a vase of flowers on her desk. She liked choosing them from the garden and arranging them whenever they needed to be changed. I had liked watching her do it from the bathroom window. Now there were dead flowers curling over the edges of the bin and she had not replaced them. A vase of green, stagnant water stood on the edge of her desk. I walked towards it and saw she had been reading through one of her lock boxes of letters. One from Mum sent to her years ago on a school field trip sat at the top.

'Darling Ellie, I'm sorry to hear the food's so yucky. Is your poor ankle feeling any better?' There was the usual coerced P.S. at the bottom from Dad – we had never understood why Mum bothered.

Then I turned around and saw Ellie's bed. Scattered inside it, crumpled where she had slept on them, were the pictures she had drawn of the dream house we planned to run away to when we were little. I recognised them straight away and picked one up – there were vines and flowers and monkeys on the roof, and a moat so no one could get in. I saw her small bunched hand holding the crayon. Beside her pillow was her little crucifix. The sheet looked stained, as if she had wet the bed – and I realised that was what was causing the smell. I pushed the window open and sat on the chair waiting for the sound of the bath draining away.

She was not long. Her face looked angry and frightened.

'What are you doing in my room?' she said.

'I'm sorry, Ellie.'

'It's *my* room.'

'I know, I'm just – I'm worried about you. I thought we could have a chat or something.'

She stood still, looking at me as if she didn't understand my words and then she said,

'Please close your eyes so I can get into bed.'

I heard the towel drop on the floor and the creak of her mattress.

'I'm in,' she said. She had pulled the covers right up to her chin and she stared at me,

'Ellie, what's up?' I tried to make my voice very calm.

'I'm OK.'

'I don't think you are, really. Why's your room in such a mess? Your sheets are—'

'I don't know,' she said.

She had always come to me in the past if she was upset. Was it obvious to her what a selfish, dishonest person I had become? Perhaps she did not think it was worth coming to a person like me.

'I'm sorry, Ellie,' I told her, 'I've been thinking about myself all the time and I haven't made sure you were all right.'

She looked away at the opposite wall for a moment, her eyes tightening over a thought.

'Well, it's not like it's your job, is it?'

'It doesn't have to be my job. I love you, Ellie. You're my sister.'

'Em, I think I normally am all right,' she said, 'but I might not be at the moment.' Her voice was very quiet.

'No,' I said. 'Has something bad happened?'

She nodded and started to cry and I sat on the floor by her bed and stroked her hair.

'Can you say what?'

'I don't know if I can say.'

Fear is a flash of white light sometimes – a stranger taking your photograph, locking you into a moment against your will. Had something bad happened? The way 'something' had gone wrong to stop Simon calling? The air was full of nameless threats, bigger than all promises, all trust. I felt her soft hair under my fingers – soft as Simon's hair. I closed my eyes. When we were little, I used to sing to her sometimes, when she got scared. 'Daisy, Daisy,' 'There's a hole in my bucket' – anything predictable, repetitive would calm her.

I used to tell myself she was always getting scared for no reason. But I always knew that wasn't true, really. She got scared because things felt wrong in our house – tampered with. Life felt the way a room might feel if you came back into it and everything had been moved an inch to the left, and everyone pretended nothing was wrong. There were nameless threats – they were what we all felt. There were those threats that drove Dad to sleep in the spare room, to slam the door of his study after supper each night. There were those that sent Mum out to church every day or to scream 'Get out!' so hard her voice cracked, at an au pair girl with too many boyfriends. And for me there was always that strange cry from Irena's kitchen and the look that passed between me and Tomasz, acknowledging it. Is this life, that look said, this sitting in the hallway, waiting, unable to interpret the signs?

'Ellie, shall we wait a bit – and talk about it later?' I said. I wanted to escape and I knew it. The house had shrunk around me.

'I think I'll get dressed first,' she said. She pulled the covers off, forgetting about my presence this time, and I saw scratch marks down her arms and her skinny back. Without her clothes and her make-up, she is still a child.

'I'll come back in a minute, then – when you're dressed.'

I walked into the hall, and wondered how long my phone had been ringing. I answered it this time – feeling glad to speak to anyone. It was Ronnie, wanting to know where Tom was.

'How should I know where he is? Why does everyone ask me about Tom?' I said. I knew he would not understand the fear in my voice. 'Look, we've split up, Ronnie.'

'Shit, Em – when did all this happen?'

'Oh, about five or six days ago.' I could hardly remember, it was so unimportant to me now. Do all people just throw each other away, like rubbish? How little I had deserved that love Tom showed in his face, in those tense hands of his gripping the steering wheel, when he last dropped me home.

'But anyway, you saw him yourself, Ronnie – didn't he say anything about me and him?' I said. I knew Tom's pride would have been too great to mention Simon. But I suddenly hoped that at least he had been able to talk to his friends about how

I had let him down. As Andrea said, he was very vulnerable. I hated myself, and now that hatred mixed with dread of what had upset Ellie – as if I had hurt her myself.

And when I look back over the story now, I know that I did hurt her myself. Will I go on throughout my life expecting blame to present itself to me immediately, a policeman with his hand up, preventing all further damage? Blame is self-contained, oblivious to time – it is there waiting in your own mind, when you are ready to read it.

'What d'you mean, babe?' Ronnie said. 'I haven't seen Tom all week. Oh, what – the other night, when Sarah and I called you? No, man, he didn't turn up. We thought we spotted him in a taxi, but it was someone else. His phone's been off since. You know Tom – he can't be on his own five minutes. I'm kind of worried about him, Em.'

'Look I'm sorry, Ronnie, I'm the last person to ask where Tom is at the moment,' I said.

When we finished talking I found myself leaning out of the window, looking over towards Andrea's house. I was remembering Tom's face as he stood looking at me and Simon together – the quiet acceptance on it that had seemed despairing and brutal at once. It was as if that kind of betrayal was what he expected of the world – he seemed unshockable, immune to cruelty. It frightened me, like that unmentioned sister of his, like the way he had bullied Kate on the roof at Jamie's. Like the memory of my cheek crushed against the car window, his angry face above me. I never want to see him again, I thought.

'Em?' Ellie said. She had come up behind me. I turned around and put my arms out and she let me hug her. I felt her tears soaking through my T-shirt. After a while she stopped crying and through her quick breath I heard her say the word Tom. It was like the moment you hit the ground in a dream of falling.

'What about him, Ellie?'

'The other night – when I stayed out . . .'

'Were you with Tom's friends?' I said. Now it seemed like the only explanation. I had known she and her friends would not stay out all night together.

'No, not his friends. Just him,' she said. And then she told me what had happened.

Tom had got her drunk, stoned, showed her how to do lines of coke. At first Ellie smiled as she was telling me – she had loved it in the club, she said, she felt like a film star. And people really believed she was eighteen. Could I believe one man said he thought she was about twenty-two? And then Tom told her she was pretty, but she didn't believe he meant that.

'I know I'm not beautiful like you,' she told me. Her eyes looked at me dreamily for a moment – sadly.

Time went so fast, she said. They were dancing – Tom kept disappearing and she would be dancing on her own or some other man would dance up against her – and then he would come back and she could not tell if she had blinked or if it had been half an hour. She thought maybe he was getting more drinks for himself or having more coke. He really loved the coke, she said – he licked it up and rubbed it all over his gums like he was pretending to brush his teeth. It had made her laugh and he told her to shut up or he would take her home because maybe she was too young to be out that late.

Then the place closed and they were outside. He told her

to come with him down a little side street for a minute just to see something and then they stopped and he started to kiss her and he put his hand inside her T-shirt. She was scared, but he kept saying it didn't matter, that everyone did it the whole time and it meant nothing to any of them. 'Emily loves it,' he told her.

So she just closed her eyes. They were up against a wall, and the bricks scratched her arms and her back. It hurt – it hurt so much she said she thought she would scream the next second, then the next, then the next. She said it seemed to take for ever.

'I think I'm going to go to hell now,' she told me.

And when he dropped her off, he just stopped the car and said nothing. He waited for her to get out. She got her leg caught in the seat belt and fell on to the road on her knees. He leant over and pulled the door shut, then he reversed the car away. I remembered hearing the sound of the car – looking at Mum in the sitting room, just seconds before Ellie put her key in the lock.

People say you lose faith in the world gradually. It ebbs away – that's a phrase I have heard people use. Only in ancient times, in stories, did the heart actually break. Uncle Peter told me a story once. I was six or seven, sitting on his lap. There was a cigarette in his fingers, the lamp through the smoke. Perhaps it was Christmas. This is the story of how a sea got named, he said.

'Aegeus was an old king who had a son named Theseus. This old king loved his son more than anything in the world, Emily. But Theseus was young and ambitious. Everyone in the kingdom was telling stories of a terrible monster overseas called the Minotaur. One day Theseus decided he would be the one to kill it. He sailed away in a beautiful big ship – as people often do.' He tapped his cigarette, sighed, held me close. That was Peter.

'Before Theseus left, he and his father had made an agreement: when the ship comes back, black sails means you are dead, white sails you are still alive. Now all old Aegeus could do was wait. He waited years at the window – years and years – for that ship to come back into the harbour.'

Peter looked down at me. I remember him whispering in my ear as if he was telling me a secret:

'Can you imagine, Emily, an old man's whole life and happiness all depending on the colour of some sails? It's a strange old world, isn't it?

'Anyway, far away from his dad, life had got complicated for Theseus. Something went wrong – something no one could have predicted. He hurt a girl's feelings. He didn't love her. And the girl cried and cried. She put a curse on Theseus: make him forgetful, Gods, she said.

'Theseus thought no more about her. Why worry – these things happen. He found the monster and fought and killed him. And so Theseus sailed for home, victorious – alive. His old Dad would be so happy, so proud, he thought.

'But in all his excitement, Emily, he forgot one thing. He forgot to change the black sails for white. And as his old father watched that beautiful ship sail back into the harbour, sun on the water, black sails flapping, he died of a broken heart. He fell into the deep sea. They named it after him, the Aegean Sea they called it.'

'Peter, that's a pretty funny story to tell a little girl,' Dad said.

'Is it?'

There was rain outside the window, Mum drawing the curtains, I think.

A funny story to tell a little girl. Why? Because it was a threat to my innocence? Don't tell the young about black sails, deep seas. It was no stranger than the story of my parents' marriage. Or the story of Andrea and Tony, of Stefan and Irena. Or the story of Tom and Simon and Ellie and me.

I saw Ellie's bright face in the mouth of that alleyway. I heard Tom's words:

'Come with me for a minute – just to see something?' The casualness of the words, the lack of persuasion. It was as if he knew she would follow, whatever he said. I put Ellie into my bed and put a scarf over the lampshade so that she would not be in the dark. Not in that deep sea.

I waited for her to go to sleep and then I went down to the kitchen and looked at the moon on the floor. It was like a little puddle of water on the tiles. I went out into the garden and lay on the grass and looked up at the dim stars. An aeroplane went slowly across the sky. I could feel the earth caking up under my fingernails and tears going round the back of my neck.

I watched the sky right through the night, until it started to get lighter. I listened to the sounds changing by the hour: first the cats, and the trees blowing, then the cars starting up again. I heard windows coming up, children's voices, a radio. The sun came out and I could smell coffee and bacon. Ants crawled over my hands.

My mind went back to the first time Tom and Ellie had

met. The way he had tickled her and her T-shirt twisted up and her knickers were showing. I could hardly bear to think of him touching her, but the filthy image was in my mind – his hand on her stomach, tickling her more, the orange juice knocked into the sink, glugging down the drain. The pattern on her knickers – little pink pigs running in all directions.

'I'm going to tickle you and tickle you until I make you wet yourself,' he told her. And what did I do? I ran upstairs with the rubbish bag, not knowing what I was running away from, or not wanting to know, and I met Simon on the street and forgot all about them for a while.

I could not believe I had left them alone together. I could not believe the extent of my selfishness, my blindness to Tom's anger.

And there was the time I had come back from spying on Simon and Rachel and found Tom and Ellie playing cards in the kitchen. What was Tom doing there? I hadn't even questioned it at the time.

'Your little sister's a shark,' Tom said. 'There's a vicious streak somewhere in your family.'

'There is not,' Ellie said. 'I'm just cleverer than you. People aren't being vicious just because you lose – don't you know that?'

Had she understood him before I had? Had she already seen that furious indignation in him which seemed to make him feel he had the right to do anything?

There were such similarities in our backgrounds: the spoilt marriages, the unhappiness in our families and the strategies for avoiding it – whether it was by moving house endlessly or just by keeping quiet. Maybe I feel disappointed, I thought, but Tom feels wronged – and that is far more dangerous.

I sat up and shook the leaves out of my hair and went up to see Ellie. I lay down beside her and slept for a while. She put her arms round me and buried her face in my hair. Her breath was soft and whistling, like a little baby. Sometimes I feel as though I am her mother.

I woke up late in the morning and got up softly to let her sleep as long as she could. I put on clean clothes – whatever was lying around my room. I did not want to open the wardrobe and see that red dress. I went downstairs. Dad keeps whisky in the cupboard on the landing. I took a long drink from the bottle. It felt like disinfectant in my throat, my brain. Like father, like daughter, I thought.

In my mother's room (why call it my parents' room, when I know perfectly well she sleeps alone in there?) there is a framed poster with the words of some saint or holy person on it:

'All shall be well and all shall be well and all manner of thing shall be well.' I sat on her neat bed, with its smell of lavender, the folded handkerchief by the pillow, and read the meaningless words a few times. Where did her certainty come from that love was about never causing people pain? Even Mum's safe, sanitised love for Dad had caused pain to him, to me and Ellie, to Mum herself.

Just then, pain seemed limitless – and unavoidable. People's lives seemed to be constructed of nothing but dirty coincidence. Why had I met Tom at Sarah's party? Why had our parents known each other? Why was Andrea's new house opposite my bedroom window and why had Simon been there to decorate it?

Now, when I look back more quietly, I see one 'why' which seems to stretch far behind the others, into the past. Why had the chance facts of so many lives led, like a complex mathematical formula, to that combination of Tom's anger and Ellie's insecurity in a back street behind a club? Because, when I think about it, it is set up like an answer to something: a + b + c + d + e + f = x{y}, where x is Tom and {y} is Ellie with her eyes closed tightly.

I went downstairs. On the coffee table in the sitting room was the vase Mum and I had smashed when we carried Ellie up the stairs. She had found every piece and glued it back together. It sat drying neatly on a folded piece of newspaper. I imagined smashing it again. Then I picked up Dad's car keys from the hall table and went out to look for Tom.

Chapter eleven

I drove around west London, to all the cafés and bars I knew Tom went to in the day. The routines of his life repulsed me; his daily round of coffees and magazines and cigarettes with friends. New trainers, new CDs, a new kind of cappuccino. Each place had been chosen to say something about him: arty, bohemian, slick – the sunshine slanted on the metal tables, the geometric black-and-white photos hung along the walls. They were film sets – like all the places he had taken me to – full of young people convinced by the same magazines, the same TV that all the world wanted was a close-up of them.

Behind each glass door there were just strangers – the wrong face like a slap, shining empty tables where he ought to have been. I saw no one I knew, not one of his friends. It was as if they were all conscious this was a special day, a day when it was best to stay safe at home. I looked around at the people with their sandwiches and coffee and I wanted to tell them to go home too.

I suppose I must have looked crazy. People glanced round as I rushed along the street. I didn't care. It's happened, I wanted to say. Fat man with glasses, woman with a pushchair, old lady crossing the road – do you know what's happened to my sister? She's been hurt and really it's my fault. She's only a baby. She likes me to sit outside her room when she goes to sleep. I got bored and went away and she must have got scared – the cot smashed down and now she won't stop crying.

But that was not it this time. Each time I remembered, I thought I would be sick. I wondered how I had moved and breathed between remembering. Then the lights would change, or a dog barked on its lead and I forgot just enough to go on to the next place, to find Tom.

While I drove I called his mobile again and again, ringing off at the familiar intake of breath at the start of his answer-phone message. The repeated sounds ran together, became panting and I remembered his teeth biting down on his lower lip, his eyes closing slowly on the car seat underneath me, the scratches on Ellie's back, where he had pushed her up against a brick wall. My mouth was dry, my hands shook on the steering wheel, I cried and rubbed my face on my sleeve. I must have let the car slow down to a halt – a lorry driver sounded his horn at me from behind. A big angry god in a huge machine. The loud noise went right through me, through my nails, my hair. But I want to slow down, I thought. I felt a great desire to slow down.

At last there was only Andrea's old house to try. Tom never

stayed at home – as Ronnie said, he couldn't be on his own for five minutes. In fact, it was hard to imagine him alone at all. He seemed to me then to have drawn his whole existence out of other people's reactions to his beauty, his clothes, his generosity at the bar. This would be my last contribution to it.

I stopped the car at the top of their road. Perhaps Simon would be there – with Rachel, I thought. They had probably caught the train back from Edinburgh together. I could see them in their seats beside the speed-blurred landscape, sobered, holding hands, perhaps. But I didn't care. I can face anything, I thought, so long as I can look Tom in the eye. What did I think I could do – knock him out cold with my *eyes*?

I walked across the lawn through the bright sunshine. The dry grass gave out a strong smell of hay and the flowers looked dry as sticks. There were four cars parked in the driveway – one of them Simon's, the others I didn't recognise. Andrea obviously had people over.

The front door stood open – there were balloons tied to the door handle. Red, green and yellow, the bright colours shocking as laughter. I walked into the hallway and stopped. I could hear a mixer going in the kitchen, saucepans clanked in a cupboard.

'Serena?' someone called. 'We're thinking half two for lunch. Will the kids last that long?'

'Oh sure, I think so. They've had crisps and so on, haven't they – they'll live.'

It was Rachel's voice – the other one must have belonged to one of the guests. That warm American accent which always sounds false to me, I thought – their sugary cakes baking, their handguns in the drawer. But for all my spite, I was too frightened to go up the stairs to Tom's room. I felt dangerously out of place – hadn't I set off just a little while ago on a wonderful journey, full of hope? Did someone forget to wake me – because now I had opened my eyes somewhere strange, completely alone. I stood still, looking at the rug under my feet. Little coloured horses running, jumping through forests, over walls, through water. It was terrifying.

Then the door to the kitchen opened and Rachel came into the hallway. She had a vase of flowers in her hand. For a moment she looked like a bride.

How long did we stare at each other for? We were strangers, but hatred was a kind of intimacy between us. We did not know how to behave.

'Emily,' she said. Her voice was cool and thin as water. At first I could not speak. She continued to stare at me and I could feel her composure building, like a third person – a responsible adult – coming into the hall.

'I've only come to see Tom,' I told her.

She walked behind me and put the vase of flowers on the table in the hall window. Her slim brown hands shook the stems out, arranging them. She put the larger flowers near the back, the smaller ones at the front. I watched the pattern growing. A little shower of yellow petals fell on her shoe. Then she turned around.

'Emily, listen, it's Andrea's birthday,' she said, 'the whole family's here.'

The idea she must have had in mind – that I was going to shout, beg, accuse, in front of whoever was there – exhausted me. (Is it possible to be morally exhausted?) The things I must have done, be doing in her mind, I thought. I wished I could steal my image back out of it, out of Simon's. How desperately I had wanted to be known, understood – and then suddenly I wanted all of myself back.

I watched her bend down to collect the yellow petals. She picked them up one by one and dropped them into her cupped hand.

'*Please,* there isn't a scene in me, Rachel. I've just come to see Tom.'

'A *scene*?' She laughed. 'God, you were so sure he'd tell me, weren't you?'

I stared at the little horses on that rug and tried not to imagine how much she must hate me. I felt it, though, like the blast from an oven door. She tossed the petals into the bin and brushed her hands off neatly over it.

'Did you *really* think he'd leave me? I'm interested to know.'

'Yes,' I said. 'I did.' There was no point in lying, no point in apologising. I had wanted to win.

'Really?' The word twitched in a spasm across her face.

'Yes.' I felt the absence of that belief like a bereavement now.

'But we're *married,* Emily.' She stood up and laid her hand on the wooden table. Her fingers were brown and long on the polished wood.

'I know.'

'You think *marriages* break up that easily? A girl, a little girl comes along . . .'

I felt humiliated by her composure – her legitimacy. I wanted to smash it up, like that vase Mum had glued together –

'It does happen you know, Rachel. People fall in love,' I said – and as I said it I knew it was possible to hate the sound of your own voice.

She looked right at me.

'In *love?* As if you're the only one.'

'I don't believe you,' I said.

I had underestimated her. I had never really counted her will into my calculations, now there it was in front of me, the largest factor of all. It had made her anger greater than her pride – she preferred to have me believe Simon was repeatedly unfaithful to her, than that I was special in any way. She amazed me. She smiled falsely, violently and flicked her hair off her shoulders.

'But you have no reason to disbelieve me, Emily. *I've* never lied to you.'

A burst of laughter from the drawing room was like the slap of the sea on a cabin window – and I could hardly raise my head for sickness. Rachel leant back on the table for a moment, an expression of casual thoughtfulness on her face.

'Your parents have a fuck-up of a marriage, right? They're basically divorced,' she told me. 'It's kind of a joke with Andrea and Tony that they still live in the same house together. But who are they to laugh? Or Simon's parents, for that matter. They're divorced too, like *everyone* else in this family.' She sighed and looked out of the window.

'What does it do to the kids, really? Tell me. See, I'm from a stable background and it's kind of hard for me to understand. Does it make you think promises don't matter? Don't you *believe* in anything?'

I looked away – she was like an angry flower in the corner, hateful and vicious in her pretty dress. I thought about what Mum had said: 'Let yourself believe in a few things, Emily.'

'Did Simon tell you his parents are divorced too?'

'No,' I said.

'He can't even talk about it, it scares him so much.'

Her superiority, her supernatural calmness astounded me. How could anyone have argued with it – breathed beside it at night? I wanted to tell her Simon had said he loved me. No argument, no hospital bed, none of the blackmail she had used. Even that first time I met her, when Simon had come to talk to me on the kitchen step, she had blackmailed him. I remember how her neat face slightly tightened, her soft voice said, 'Simon, would you mind getting me some painkillers?'

And he flinched – as though that will of hers had actually stepped out of her and hit him:

'Have you got a headache, darling?'

Couldn't I at least ruin her illusions for her? I had nothing – surely no one would begrudge me that. But what was the point? She was not my enemy really – Simon's fear was. Tom's anger. I had done her enough harm – and I had done enough harm to myself. I watched her finger trace the inlaid pattern on the wooden table.

'You know, maybe I should *thank* you, Emily,' she laughed and rolled her eyes: 'maybe this whole thing with you brought Simon full circle – back to what he believes in. Because when he was crying and begging me to forgive him, I thought, yeah – you've remembered you're lucky; you broke the pattern with me.'

Crying and begging her to forgive him. I could not hold

him together as one person in my mind – all those contradictions at war with each other, I thought. But was it really such a surprise? I could barely hold myself together, either –

'For Christ's sake,' I said, 'it's not a pattern. People have free will.' Did she really think she could arrange people the way she had arranged those flowers?

'Not a pattern?' She laughed again. 'But look around you, look at *yourself* – kind of disgraceful, desperate in someone else's hallway.'

Her words seemed to hang in the air through several seasons. At last I looked away, as if I expected to see Tomasz by the stairs, his eyes watering, knowing. Hatred is accurate, I thought.

'Look, I'm going in,' she said. 'Tom's over at the new house, Emily, so why don't you just go there?'

She stopped with her fingers on the sitting-room door handle and looked at me, deciding something. Then she pushed the door wide open. The light flashed out. Breeze blew through from the windows at the end of the room. There was music – a woman smiling, head on one side, playing the piano. People sat around on sofas. Two little girls played with wrapping paper on the floor. There were glasses of champagne, plates of bread and smoked salmon. A faint smell of women's perfume.

A middle-aged man in a suit stood up.

'Rachel!' he called out. He spread his arms wide, his mouth wide, 'what a *stunning* dress.'

I watched her hug and kiss him. Simon got up from the chair beside them. His feet moved carefully round a glass of champagne on the carpet then his smiling face turned towards the doorway, not knowing what it was about to see. The smile went. I remembered him catching sight of me behind the door in the street light the night it all started. He had just come in to check the window was closed, Tom was waiting in the hall. I suppose that was what I always was to Simon – the thing he had not expected to see.

'Oh *Joe*!' Rachel laughed, 'you've cut your *hair*. All your boyish curls.' She put her hand up to the man's head. She was clever – ruthless in her unhappiness as I had been in happiness. She means to give Simon long enough, I thought – to see me looking kind of disgraceful, desperate in someone else's hallway. I could not really blame her.

'Don't you love me any more?' the man asked her. She giggled. He pouted. They were like figures in a nightmare.

Then a woman backed over to the door, looking away, nodding, talking to one of the little girls. 'What about doing a lovely drawing, darling?' she was saying. Her hand went out blindly for the door handle and she pushed it, not knowing what she was shutting out. We know so little about other people's lives. We are all like that butterfly in the desert, flapping its wing, sending out a hurricane. As the door swung slowly, I watched Simon's face. His eyes narrowed. In the thin gap of bright light against the door frame, he mouthed,

'I'm sorry.'

The little words banged into my chest. The door clicked shut.

I leant back against the table, feeling weightless. It was dim in the hallway. There was a sickening smell of meat roasting. My eyes closed. Slow down, I thought – as if I was still driving, as if that lorry driver was still sounding his horn.

Then I walked out into the garden, along the path. There was a damp feeling coming from the dried-out leaves, the yellowing grass. A sprinkler hissed and spun water in fine arcs in the corner of my eye.

I started the car. It had not occurred to me Tom would be at the new house. Hadn't it disappeared? I suppose I had imagined it would not be needed now that Simon would not be there waiting for me. The champagne, the music, the little girls with the wrapping paper . . . a birthday. How neatly life folds round, grows over.

'Life goes on' – as Uncle Peter used to sigh, when he lit one of his little cigars after supper. It all goes on, because there are a million instincts for survival built into us. Perhaps, like the body, the mind only feels one source of pain at a time. As I drove away, I felt a strange kind of freedom. Perhaps I would not hate Rachel any more now. Perhaps grief for Ellie, for Simon and myself had sapped the hate out of me. I hope it is gone for good, I thought, because anything is better than the monotony of hatred, than days spent like an addict, hoarding words, images for the dull fix of pain.

I put the car back where I had found it and walked across the road to Andrea's new house. The front door was wide open and I walked into the familiar hallway, into all the smells of paint and varnish that had waited for me each night. It all smelt so new. I called out the wrong name.

'Tom?' There was no answer. 'Tom?' I shouted. My voice was weak and flat. It was not like my voice – it was a voice calling for water, for another pillow. I did not want to sound like that in front of him.

He came through from the kitchen, his trainers soft as cats' feet on the floor. His face was thinner. He stood in front of me in his ironed shirt, clean shaven for his mother's birthday. A good boy, suddenly – making up to her, helping out after all the trouble he had caused what with the car and worrying everyone staying out so late at night. I looked at the new trainers on the floorboards. He shifted his weight. My whole body was shaking. Tears blurred the shoes over, the brown hand – the fingers picking at his thumb.

'*What*?' he said.

I looked up at him. His voice was cruel and sarcastic. His mouth was pale with anger.

'What, Emily? Simon doesn't love you?' I watched his hand twitch, pick convulsively at its own nails. Then it lifted and shot out at me. It slapped my face with a crack.

Now, when I think about that moment, I am surprised by how immediately I accepted his reaction. But what was there for him to say after all? What was there for me to say? We were as far apart as two people can be. All our attempts at communication had proved misleading. Sex, laughter – we had inverted intimacy and now there was nothing to cover the white distance but his fist.

'My *sister*, Tom,' I said – again the words came out choking, weak.

'Your sister?' And again his hand shot out, against my cheek, tearing a handful of hair off with it. He threw my hair away like dirt.

There was blood in my mouth and I spat it on to the floor. I stared at him for a moment, at his blank face. He shocked me – his existence shocked me after what he had done. His good looks were obscene to me now – unscarred as they were by any of what had happened. Those looks, that false, oiled demeanour, learnt from his father, that had drawn my sister down an alleyway.

'She's a child, Tom. You've hurt a child. D'you understand that?'

He stared. Nothing.

Oh, just go, I told myself, run back home. Go back to Ellie. What had I imagined he could say that would make any difference to her?

I turned away and walked towards the door. But as I reached it he grabbed my arm, twisting it backwards. I felt faint with the fear and pain. All I could see was blank wall – white distance.

'Why don't you say you're sorry, Emily?' he said.

And suddenly it was as if the fear disappeared altogether. The words of a spoilt child: say you're sorry. As if I had taken his ball – give it *back*. Give my happiness back.

There was no space for any emotion except his anger, his indignation – perhaps there never had been, in all our time together. Perhaps it was his anger which had moved in between us when we had sex in his car, making us more and more lonely with each kiss. Say you're sorry; I heard myself laughing at him. A hard, crazy laugh. The sound of it was something remembered . . . a bright yellow bird caught in a room in France, when we were younger. Blue shutters. A yellow flash and the terrified chirruping. It circled and circled, missing the window and we watched, helpless. It knocked itself dead on the window frame.

He threw me forwards into the empty room off the hallway. I ran hard into the opposite wall, blood and saliva smearing on the new white paint. I looked at him where he had stayed on the other side of the room. He sank down against the door, on his haunches, looking at his hands – as if he couldn't believe what they had been doing. He lifted his eyes to me again, to check.

'You should look like that,' he said, 'that's my blood on you.'

I wished I could bring myself to laugh at him again. It was the cruellest thing I could do to him – more painful than his fists were to me and I knew it.

'You've hurt a child, Tom,' I said, 'someone who knew nothing about any of this. Why? Why would you hurt *Ellie*?'

'Oh, maybe she's a slut like you, Em.'

Then I was crying again. I could not stop. Come with me for a minute, I thought. Does everyone meet those words at some point in their lives? Who had first said them to me?

'Oh, let me out, Tom. I just want to get out of here.'

He leant back hard against the door.

'Why is it always Simon? My whole life. It's like there are people sent to torture you. Did you know or something – did you choose him deliberately?'

'Don't be so pathetic. It wasn't about you.' I hated his egotism all the more because I had seen it in myself. I spat on the floor again, wiped my mouth. I could feel my hand throbbing where it had slapped into the wall. Two of the fingers looked wrong. Tom seemed not to have even heard me speak.

'It's *always* him.' He shook his head, his mind far away. 'Coming to stay with us in the holidays because his parents were too fucking poor to go away. Hitting cricket balls with

Dad. Swimming races with Julia. Cooking with Mum – he was always hanging around the kitchen with her. Fuck, sometimes it was like I never ate anything without him touching it first.'

– I thought of Simon's hands, Tom's face coming down to kiss me, the smell of that meat roasting at Andrea's, the taste of blood in my mouth. You're hysterical, I told myself. I felt the horrible laughter building up in me again. I could feel my cheek swelling – I put my hand up to it and the skin felt hot.

'Are you in love with him?' he said.

'What does it matter now, Tom?'

'I don't know. Doesn't it matter? What does matter, Emily?'

Then there was silence for a second. I looked out of the window and saw a man on a bike ride past, a red shopping bag swinging on his arm.

'Ellie,' I said. Ellie – the innocent party.

Was it a funny story to tell a little girl – the one Peter told me about the deep sea? I see Dad's face looking quizzically at him and I feel confused. I can't think of another moment when Dad seemed concerned about protecting my innocence. I see him straightening his hair in the car mirror outside Irena's house, putting his hand on her knee under her kitchen table . . .

I suppose I always thought I was protecting Ellie's innocence – pretending I couldn't hear anything when she asked if that sound was Mum crying. But what had it been like for her to grow up not knowing what was wrong? Whose job is it to protect the innocent? Maybe it is no one's. Come with me for a minute, or Simon's gentle 'Come here' – maybe we are all waiting to be asked, waiting to ask each other.

Tom looked up, his face softened, sad looking,

'And me, do *I* matter?'

He was repulsive to me. I would like to have hit him the way he had hit me.

'No. Not after what you've done. You're not even human to me any more.'

'Neither are you, Emily. You're just – nothing.'

So there we stood: a boy and a girl meaning nothing to each other.

And then he came at me. He held my head back against the wall and he punched my face hard – once. I remember the sound of his arm swinging through the air. And I remember my legs folding, the floor rising up to meet my cheek, the warm curtain of blood over my mouth, the dark red drops on the floor. My red dress, I thought . . .

It is getting dark now. I have not moved. For now I want to lie here, irresponsible, my body just how it fell away from Tom's fist.

When Simon lay next to me in here, I would look over at his body, pale and slim in the street light – and I would call it mine. I used to throw my arms round his neck, pull him against me. 'You're mine, all *mine*,' I would say, and we would laugh at that silly behaviour, not fearing the ironies we were throwing so far ahead. Mine, all mine – what a thing to claim. I look at my arm now, where it fell independently, an object bent back behind my head. Do I even possess that arm?

Of course we never own each other. And when even our own outlines shift, when we do the unexpected, the unplanned, we find we hardly own ourselves. Who knows why people stay together, why Dad prefers to sleep in the spare room with the dusty books, to drink his whisky from the bottle at night – a kind of baby – rather than to leave? Who knows why Simon came towards me smiling, shaking his head – 'I made a mistake. I'm young, the world won't collapse, will it? Wouldn't it be more wrong to stay with her now?' – and the next day he was crying and begging Rachel to forgive him. Marriage runs very deep, my mother said. As deep as loneliness? For my parents – even for Simon and Rachel – I hope so. But I do not think it does.

I should go back and check on Ellie. If only for her, I will not lie here kind of disgraceful, desperate any more. I must clean up, wash the blood off my face so I don't scare her.

I wonder what my face looks like – there are no mirrors here. I hope it looks different.

The cold water feels good on my hand, on my face. I'll let the tap run for a second over my swollen eye. There is nothing to dry my face on. The air feels almost cold on my wet skin – like the feeling of the little cross shape Mum used to draw on my head with the holy water. I remember how it stood out like metal for a few seconds in that cold air in the church. I remember how I felt I had been marked with a magic stamp. She would dip her fingers in the font and lift my chin. The aisle was enormous to me under her arm, stretching far away to the other world of the altar.

I would like to have some holy water now. Does tap water work? I don't think tap water is holy, though. It makes me smile now, to think of all those silly things we used to ask Mrs Faulkner in the first Communion class – 'Does God live with Father Christmas?', 'Is His bed made of clouds?' She was a kind woman, really, her words always glittery somehow like words in a fairy tale. Some words in particular . . . something about believing even if no one is around to help you, even if people make fun of you (Mrs Faulkner was always imagining people would make fun of us).

'Jesus went up into the hills to pray,' she read to us. 'When evening came He was there alone.'

– I remember the blank children's faces, the smell of milk and biscuits, the scared look of the little boy who always wet himself. Someone pinched my arm and giggled. I think we drew pictures that day: God's big, invisible hand holding our families. I lost mine somewhere in the cloakroom – but I suppose those words have stayed all this time. Who knows why we remember the things we do? My mind is full of them – no matter how hard I have tried to empty it.

And these rooms will be full of furniture soon. Andrea's things, heavy with her life. The colourful rug she and Tony bought on holiday, the glasses that were a wedding present. I can imagine them, picture her unpacking it all in here. I can see her face – melancholy, determined in its heavy make-up, moving on.

I have always liked an empty room. Sometimes I used to wish Mum and Ellie and I could move, buy just a few things – all very new and clean. Simon laughed at me once for that. I said I liked this house the way it was, I liked things simple – and he laughed at me. But I will not cast him in the role of sophisticate – he was as innocent and stupid and as dangerous as I was, in his own way. Had he been brought full circle, as Rachel said, back to what he believed in – or just safely away from what he didn't? All I know is, lying in there with him at night, trying to believe the incredible had happened, that love might last, there were moments when the emptiness of that room was all I could feel. I believe that Simon is sorry.

It didn't rain after all. It's another hot night. The garden gate creaks into it as I push it shut behind me. I wonder if I will always hear that sound as they come in and out. Will I hear it suddenly while I am brushing my hair and think: Simon, the way I did when a car pulled up outside, when the doorbell rang, when footsteps slowed painfully under my window. Simon, Simon. Or will the sound drop out of significance imperceptibly, like the door to the spare room closing each night, like my mother crying – and become part of the sound of traffic.

I wonder where Irena is now.

The light is on in my bedroom window. Maybe Ellie is still curled up in my bed. I will get in with her and go to sleep like when we were little.

'I can't wait till I'm older,' she once told me, 'I think I'll fall in love.'

And when it is evening and you find you are alone, will you hate – like Tom, like Dad, like Andrea? I will not hate. At least I will not hate.